J.S. Andrews was born in B[...] and a French mother. He [...] Lancashire. Ever since his fi[...] for him an unquenchable fa[...] a variety of boats and sea-go[...]

He began writing technical articles and cruising stories for the yachting press at the age of thirty-one, but with an interest in history and archaeology inspired by his grandfather, Sydney Andrews, and broadened and shared since he married, it is not surprising that his first novel should be about the distant past of Strangford Lough on which he so often sails near his home.

THE BELL OF NENDRUM

J.S. Andrews

THE
BLACKSTAFF
PRESS

BELFAST AND DOVER, NEW HAMPSHIRE

First published in 1969
by The Bodley Head
This Blackstaff Press edition is a photolithographic
facsimile of the first edition printed
by C. Tinling & Co. Ltd.

This edition published in 1985
by The Blackstaff Press
3 Galway Park, Dundonald, Belfast BT16 0AN, Northern Ireland
and
51 Washington Street, Dover, New Hampshire 03820 USA

© J.S. Andrews 1969, 1985
All rights reserved

Printed in Northern Ireland
by The Universities Press Limited

British Library Cataloguing in Publication Data

Andrews, J.S.
The bell of Nendrum.
I. Title
823'.914[F]   PR6051.N46/
ISBN 0 85640 341 5

Contents

Author's Note, 7
1. The Bay behind the Islands, 9
2. Nial, Son of Ross, 27
3. 'What is Steel?', 51
4. Outboards and Rudders, 64
5. The Treasure of Aendrum, 82
6. Lady of the Herb Garden, 93
7. The Battle of the Longship, 101
8. Boyhood Hide-hole, 120
9. Race to Give Warning, 137
10. Fire and Sword, 160
11. 'Those who run away . . .' 181
12. 'Perhaps in other times . . .' 189

Author's Note

> '*A.D. 974* Sedna Ua Demain, Abbot of Aendruim,
> was burned in his house.'
>
> *Ancient Irish Document*

This book is the result of an actual happening.

In the year A.D. 974, the monastery situated on the island of Mahee in Strangford Lough, County Down, was attacked and destroyed. Apart from one or two minor and short-lived intrusions, the greater part of the site has remained uninhabited from that time, so that today one may still see the ruins of what was once an extremely famous teaching abbey.

Between the years 1922-24 the site was excavated by the Archaeological Section of the Belfast Natural History and Philosophical Society, under the guidance of the late Mr H. C. Lawlor. From his book *The Monastery of St Mochaoi of Nendrum*, I have culled information enabling me to describe many articles mentioned in this story (the sundial, the nail-studded door of the School House, the slate 'trial pieces', drawing instruments, etc., and the Bell of Nendrum, found where it had hastily been hidden at the time of the raid), and also to recreate the characters of the Danish twins, the Norse Abbot, Bronach, and others. I have many reasons to be grateful to that and other works, such as *Early Christian Ireland* by Máire and Liam de Paor, a description of Nendrum set out by the late Reverend William Reeves, M.B., in 1845, the similar Paper *Norsemen and Danes of Strangford Lough* by D. E. Lowry (1926), and *An Archaeological Survey of County Down* published by H.M. Stationery Office in 1966.

Nendrum is there for all to see, and so, sailing from time to time on the blue waters of the lough, is *Cuan*. The story is one of life a thousand years ago—towards the end of the so-called 'Dark Ages'. And in seeing this, we hold up a mirror which in some way reflects our own astonishing existence . . .

J. S. ANDREWS

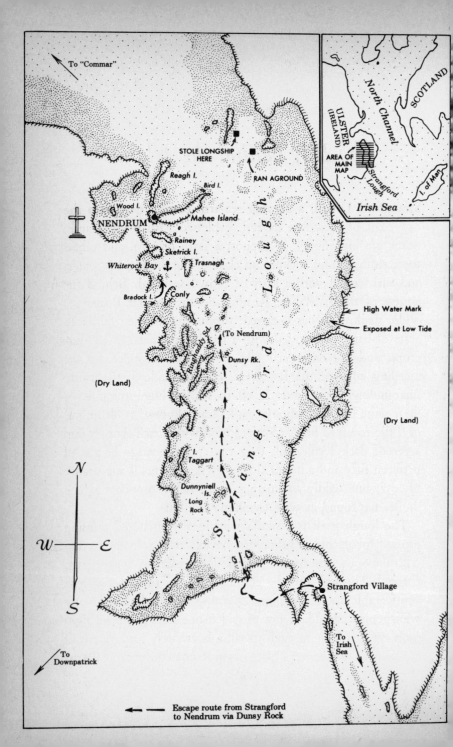

I

The Bay behind the Islands

Strangford Lough, a curving sea-arm cutting deep into the east coast of Northern Ireland, is blessed with many islands. Some are big enough to support a farm or two, and others mere stony humps sticking up clear of the shining salt waters and surrounded with a skirt of brown seaweed. Behind the largest of them, Mahee, Reagh, and the smaller Rainey, a wide, shallow bay is enclosed, turning as the tide falls into acres of bare mud dotted with a handful of islets, rocky outcrops, and the occasional pile of boulders dropped by the receding edge of the last great Ice Age. Indeed, the entire surrounding countryside is composed of huge mounds of these same boulder deposits, geologically known as 'drumlins' or 'little rounded hills'. Covered now with a rich though thin layer of dark fertile soil, they rise to an average height of between fifty and a hundred feet, giving a general appearance of low, but wildly undulating green fields, amongst which the sea has found its way, twinkling and blue.

The lough itself is nowadays an ideally sheltered cruising ground for yachts and dinghies, having as its sole connection with the open Irish Sea a five-mile-long, narrow, rock-strewn channel. Through this the ebb and flow of the tides rush at considerable speed, swirling, churning and boiling into tiny whirlpools and eddies; but provided one does so at the right moment, it is easy enough to sail a boat safely into or out of the lough. Up these very Narrows in Roman times came Patric, later acclaimed Patron Saint of Ireland, and in the eighth century the low, sinister shapes of Viking dragon-ships glided in from the sea, their riotous crews settling on its western shore to give the fast-flowing or 'strong' fjord its present name. The Irish at that time called it simply 'Cuan', the Harbour Lough.

Nial Ross called his 12-foot dinghy *Cuan*. Somehow the ancient name went well with her traditional construction of overlapping planks, her iron drop-keel or centre-plate, and in particular her old-fashioned lugsail rig.

To say Nial had been delighted when on the morning of his fifteenth birthday he had discovered her presence in the family garage, would have been understating the case more than a little. He was so thrilled that on almost every day of those Easter holidays he was out of the house straight after breakfast and away on the bus down to where they had chosen to keep the boat, at Whiterock on the western shore of the lough. Alongside the jetty by the white concrete-and-glass Yacht Club, he would rig *Cuan* carefully, and then sail off on his own, out between the scores of mooring-buoys and early launched yachts, until, passing close under the pale-blue stern of his parents' own cruising boat, he could bear away towards more open water, and the host of islands waiting to be explored.

At week-ends, Nial got a lift there because his parents were busily refitting their sloop for the season's sailing. Normally he would have helped to do the scrubbing and painting, but with *Cuan* being so new, his father hadn't the heart to keep him from venturing out on his own among the inlets and sounds of the lough. Time, of course, was the biggest difficulty. On week-days there was the bus to catch back to Belfast, not to mention the long, long walk up to the main road; the days were short, too. Nevertheless, Nial managed to visit most of the nearer islands, Conly, Rainey and Trasnagh; out to Roe, and down as far as Darragh. He had sailed through narrow passages where the tides ran strongly. He had strolled ashore among the deserted grasses, thistles, and brambles. *Cuan* had gone aground on some unsuspected shoal or other on several occasions, and even when it rained or was flat calm, to Nial it was as though the fresh sun and a good breeze played on him, so great was his enjoyment.

But always, long before the day's end, time ran out, prematurely shortening the distance he could cover, limiting the places he could see or sail round. There was, for instance, that bay behind Mahee. You needed the right tide for that. If only, oh, if only he could have more *time*. If he could just stay, living nearby for a mere week . . .

This thought kept entering his mind again and again during that next, long, summer term at school. Hopefully, he hinted at the subject in one or two letters home, and finally his parents consented to his spending a week alone, living in their cruiser, with the one condition that there must be no sailing either at night, or anywhere down near the strong tides of the Narrows.

It was the last Saturday in July when Nial excitedly clambered into the back of the family car among a heap of things that everyone had considered essential for reasonably comfortable self-preservation. Apart from the cooker on the yacht, he would need the little duffle bag containing the family camping gas-stove for use in *Cuan*, and there was of course a food-box, a polythene water-can, and a big Terylene sail-bag which held his bed-roll and spare clothes. A bundle of lightweight blue oilskins and a transparent plastic case containing a large-scale Admiralty Chart of Strangford Lough, a present from his father, completed the list.

The journey down to Whiterock seemed unending. His

mother talked a bit to begin with, but Nial's answers were so brief that she gave up, and let him fill his mind with anticipation of the coming days. At last the car came to a halt in the Club's dinghy park. *Cuan* was soon trundled down the slipway into the waiting water, and made fast at the jetty. Nial took care in stowing his equipment on the bottom-boards, making sure that nothing would slide when *Cuan* heeled to the pleasant little breeze blowing up from the south. It would be a beam reach, out to the sloop. He would get settled in first during the evening and perhaps go for just a short sail before turning in. His parents very carefully had not asked just where he intended to explore, which was nice of them. You never knew with adults, he thought, as he leaned over the stern to fix the rudder in place; it was likely that they would want to come to see if he was all right during the week, but it would be more fun if they did not. They seemed to have sensed this however, and didn't even look as though they intended to come out to the yacht with him.

Nial looked up, as he struggled into his lifejacket.

'Mum?'

'Yes, dear?'

'Any chocolate in the food-box?'

'Wait and see.'

'Oh good! Well, that seems to be everything! Oh, and Dad, you needn't worry, I won't be going near the Narrows and I'll always be careful and I'll not sail at night and I'll see you here on Sunday week. But don't come too early; give me the whole day!'

'O.K., son.' His father smiled to himself, watching the white sail fluttering jerkily up as Nial tugged on the halyard. 'Just a minute, before you cast off!' He went back to the car and again opened the boot—and returned with the little outboard motor that normally belonged to the yacht's inflatable dinghy. 'Here, Nial. But don't forget,' he added, lowering the engine onto the jetty, 'only use this when it's really necessary.'

'Gosh, Dad! Can I really have it?' Nial gripped the motor firmly. 'It'll make a big difference when I go in behind Mahee ... I didn't mean to tell you that!'

'I didn't hear it,' grinned his father, 'But as I say, do keep the thing for emergencies. Tank's full, but I forgot to get a spare can of petrol on the way down.'

'You did heck!' said Nial, lowering the shiny engine into *Cuan*'s stern. 'That would rather have scuppered the surprise.'

'I never thought of that! Here, ready for the painter?'

As the rope thumped down on the triangle of decking forward of *Cuan*'s mast, Nial gently pushed the craft away from the quay, lowered the heavy centre-plate, and scrambled aft to the helm. Trimming in the sail, he felt her heel and smoothly gather way.

' 'Bye Mum! 'Bye Dad! And thanks for the motor!'

'Goodbye Nial,' his mother called, 'and don't forget to feed yourself properly!'

'Are you kidding?' Nial waved, turned, flicked the long brown hair out of his eyes, and settled to the business of sailing the boat clear of the now closely packed crowd of moored yachts. There was really quite a smart breeze, but not enough to make things at all difficult. He would be out to the sloop in no time, at this speed. Above the curving sail the sky was a clear and pale blue with just a few little puffy cumulus clouds; nice and settled-looking.

He slept only fitfully that night. The strange, gently rocking surroundings, so different from the dormitory bed of past weeks, and the murmur cf distant sea-birds and exciting whispers of wavelets lapping on the other side of the thin planks by his ear, kept waking him, frequently making him stir and become alert.

Sunday dawned in a golden mist, and only the fact that he was hungry prevented Nial from having an early-morning swim. He got dressed instead, in light canvas shorts, shirt, and a blue polo-necked sweater.

It was fun cooking breakfast of bacon and eggs out in the galley by the open companion hatch, watching the sun lifting to scare away the mist, and listening to the gulls crying as the incoming tide crept over their weedy feeding-grounds.

It was, like yesterday, going to be hot. Perhaps, by the look of things, it would even attain that comparatively rare condition, Very Hot. Certainly, for it was completely calm now, the wind would not come strong.

A light but steady air was what he would really like for his journey into that big bay behind Mahee Island. The only remaining access by boat was on either side of Rainey Island. Before men built causeways from the mainland to Reagh Island and again thence onto Mahee, there had been other passages through, but now the whole area emptied and filled with the tide via those two remaining gaps. As a result the bay was silting up, so that very few people took their boats there. Today, thought Nial as he washed up, today just might be ideal for exploring it.

He collected a polythene bag containing his supply of matches, and the duffle bag in which the little camping stove was kept, and he added a pan, a tin of baked beans, loaf of bread, tin-opener, spoon, knife, a packet of cheese, three oranges and a bar of chocolate. Two bars of chocolate. That should do lunch *and* tea. He put the bag into a plastic bucket and climbed down to place it under the decking in *Cuan*'s bows, checking that the chart in its water-proof case was there also. Everything else except his lifejacket, which he wore, he left in the yacht, pulled her hatch to, and shut the cabin doors. Then, throwing his canvas sailing shoes into the bottom of the boat, he dropped down after them.

Though he glanced for a moment at the outboard motor under the stern-sheets, he cast off and settled to the oars instead, heading *Cuan* away towards Rainey Island. The moored racing and cruising yachts astern of him sat silently on their unruffled reflections, for no one was about yet.

He had gone barely a hundred yards, almost abreast of the end of Sketrick Island, which with its ruined castle formed the northern arm of Whiterock Bay, and beyond which lay Rainey, when to his delight the water darkened about him and in seconds a perfect little breeze came filling in from the south-east.

He lost no time in shipping rudder and centre-plate, and was soon making sail. Back at the helm, he hove in the sheet to quieten the flapping canvas, and *Cuan* heeled, the water chuckling in a contented way under the bow as she thrust forwards.

For the pure fun of it on this perfect morning, Nial circumnavigated Calf Islet, in the middle of the eastern entrance to the great and luring bay itself. Then with the sheet eased out, he steered close over to the Mahee side and, avoiding the shoals off the Rainey shore which were clearly marked on the chart at his feet, swept into the narrowest part. Here there was brief confusion, for the current squeezing through the tiny gap was going just fast enough to equal the speed of the gentle breeze, resulting in an apparently complete loss of wind and therefore control. But within a moment *Cuan* was clear again and swinging round to the right, still hugging the Mahee shore. Now the wind came abeam, and the little boat hustled through the water close under the ruins of the ancient monastic buildings of Nendrum.

Nial looked up at the broken walls. There wasn't much of them left now, other than the restored gable-end and the foundations of a tiny church. The low stump of the round tower that one usually found in major religious sites of the early Christian period in Ireland could be seen like the thick stub of a vast, broken pipe sticking vertically out of the ground on the top of the hill. Nial's parents, who were interested in antiquities, had once told him about it, and indeed had taken him there some time ago. But there was little enough to see, beyond the three great circles of heavy stone walling that enclosed the site. He remembered it had somehow given him a spooky feeling at the time. Further round the point of Mahee were the ivy-torn ruins of an Elizabethan castle, which Nial had clambered over with his father the day of the Nendrum visit; indeed the whole area was speckled with rather mysterious old remains of one kind or another.

However, what he wanted to do now was to explore those islands of the bay that were not joined to the mainland by causeways.

Turning *Cuan*'s tail to the wind, he ran her between the quickly covering mud-flats, following the relatively deep strip of water already stretching close up to the biggest of the isles. 'Wood I.', the chart called it, and indeed there were some trees round what had once been a farmhouse situated on the highest part, but that looked very deserted in the hazy warmth of this silent morning.

Even with the centre-plate up, *Cuan* grounded twice before he got near enough to scramble ashore over the stones, and the hot rays of the sun enfolded him as he wandered over the island. Insects buzzed and hummed in the tangle of bramble at the foot of the trees surrounding the empty farm. He took his time.

When he returned to the boat it was almost midday, and though the tide was now full in, there was such a feeling of sleepy peace about that Nial decided to stay there for lunch, and set to work on the bread and cheese and an orange. It was far too hot to cook things.

The air became heavy as he at last prepared to sail over towards the next biggest islet, which lay to the north-east.

Away close-hauled with the sail pinned in flat, the gentle breeze helped to cool him, but even then he was a lot more comfortable when he took his lifejacket and shirt off and threw them on top of the sweater already draped over the centre-thwart. He shouldn't have taken the jacket off, he knew, but the heat really was becoming frightful.

In the most dramatic way, the wind suddenly stopped.

Cuan glided to a standstill, about mid-way between the two islands, and now Nial felt the real strength of the sun. The glare from the water was fiercer than he had ever known it, and he began to feel odd and slightly dizzy. Then with a thickening haze that spread and spread, the sky rapidly began to darken.

The air was heavy and dull, dense. He had never seen or felt such a thing before, and despite himself he was becoming frightened. It was getting hard to breathe with the sheer weight of atmosphere, and he sat there, gasping, clutching the lifeless tiller in one hand and the limp sheet in the other.

With the violence of an explosion, there was a sudden, terrifying instant of back-pressure, like a vacuum, which shook and winded him and without pause was succeeded by a shrieking squall that caught the sail, wrenching the sheet from his hand and flinging *Cuan* far over until water poured in over the gunwale! Jamming the helm hard down and scrambling for the weather side in a valiant effort to right her, Nial held her round in a tight curve of rushing foam and froth. There was a ghastly moment when she heeled even further in the screaming wind, and took so much in over the side that he was sure she was going over. Then she came upright, with water sloshing deep almost up to the thwarts! He leapt forward to let fly the halyard and drop the sail before she bore off on the other tack. If she heeled once more, even a little, she would fill. But even as the sail came down he found that the wind had stopped, and in its place was only a loud hissing sound.

It took him some seconds to realise that the hissing was rain; rain that came stinging down on the bare skin of his shoulders and back, drumming on his skull, flattening his hair down over his eyes and ears, and plunking with such force not only into the sea, but into the water in the boat, as to raise with each drop a column of spray six inches high. Bail! He must bail! There was a tangle of rope round the bucket under the fore-decking, but he pulled it free, threw the duffle-bag back, and with a quick, swooshing movement, shot bucketful after bucketful over the side, and did not stop until it became worth lifting the floorboards to get the rest out.

The rain was easing, though when he glanced round to see how far he had drifted, he couldn't see the shore at all. With a floorboard up, and using an old can that he kept for the purpose, he bailed on until she was, relatively speaking, dry, and it was then that he noticed there was no sign of either his shirt or pullover. He looked under the foredeck, but only the wet-looking duffle-bag was there; he peered under the stern-sheets and even lifted the other floorboards; he scanned the grey, jiggling circle of water round the boat, but could see nothing. It occurred to him that his lifejacket had gone too. *That* would take a bit of explaining to his father!

He did find the chart, trapped in its soft, transparent cover under the outboard in the stern. But even a chart is not much use unless you know exactly where you are on it, and Nial had only a vague idea on that score. He pulled up the centre-plate, and getting the oars out from under the thwart, commenced to row towards where he hoped was either Reagh Island or Mahee. Still the rain teemed vertically down and he couldn't see more than a few yards in any direction. But it was only after a minute or so that, to his great relief, he could make out patches of seaweed, and then a stony foreshore close on the port side. With the sole idea of getting out of the bay, and back into Strangford Lough proper and waters that he knew at least a bit better than these, he rowed rapidly along, just keeping the stones in sight.

The heat, the wickedness of the sudden squall, and now this fantastic downpour, each unusual in its intensity, were enough to make him wonder what would happen next; but it was the fact that there had been absolutely no warning of any of them that had really unnerved him. He wanted more than anything to get out of there, out of the bay and away . . .

The shore was curving away from him . . . he pulled hard with his left hand to keep it in view. Water was running down his forehead and into his eyes, and he couldn't spare a hand to wipe them. The port oar caught momentarily under a clump of weed as the shore-line swung towards him again, and glancing over his other shoulder, he was about to sheer off a bit when—yes, there was land right beside—ahead—and before he could start to back-paddle there was a thump and a scrape, and *Cuan*'s bow ran up onto the thick brown wrack between a couple of very large boulders.

He lifted the oars inboard and reached for the chart. The only place he could think of where the land closed in to form such a narrow little bay was right between Reagh and Mahee, where a short causeway road joined the two together. Wiping the globules of rain from the plastic case, he peered again at the chart. Yes, this must be it. He turned and looked round to his right for the road. The rain was still heavy but easing again, yet he could see no sign of any obstruction to the waterway between the islands. Once more he studied the chart. There just wasn't anywhere else like this on it. And yet . . .

There was only one thing to do: he must get out and go along the shore until he came to that roadway. No one could miss the old ruined castle at that point; he must have grounded further along than it looked on the chart. He folded the thing and carefully stowed it away in the locker under the foredeck.

Taking one end of the painter with him, he clambered out over *Cuan*'s bows and up the slippery shore, sliding and staggering as his rubber-soled shoes failed to grip the shining weed and stones. In the midst of a confusion of briars at the edge of some rain-flattened grass above the high-water mark, grew a solid-looking old thorn tree, one twisted branch of which reached out over the beach. To this Nial made the rope fast, and then started off along the stones in the direction of the causeway.

He never came to it.

Sure enough, there was a well-worn footpath which arrived at the water's edge and obviously continued over some kind of ford at low tide, but no road. And neither was there a castle. Beyond the ford where some taller trees lined the shore, the bay opened out again. Indeed, it was not a bay, for the ebbing tide ran through it briskly, and *away* from Nial. It was a sound, leading out to the open lough! He knew he could not have gone through the narrows on either side of Rainey without knowing it, and yet all the other gaps between the various islands had been blocked off with proper solid causeways and roads years ago!

The rain at that moment renewed its vigour and pelted down with such splashing force that it hurt the already softened skin of his shoulders. Slipping on the slimy stones, Nial ran on and up the muddy path to the group of trees, where he crouched panting under the leaves of a sloping branch. Great drops plopped down from the foliage above, but it was better than that steaming deluge that had tried to drown and deafen him! Thank goodness it was warm! His rusty-red sailcloth shorts clung clammy and dripping to him, so that the steel sailing knife in his pocket, with its marlin spike and shackle-opener, felt heavy against his thigh. He gave the waist-band a hitch, and wondered where the devil he *could* be. Glancing at his waterproof wristwatch, he saw it was nearly two o'clock.

'That will be the fairing shower.'

Nial jumped as though he had leant on something hot. The voice had been matter-of-fact, but he had seen no one. A strange, lean, hooded figure appeared slowly from round the trunk of the tree. Nial opened his mouth and stared. The figure smiled pleasantly.

'I had no wish to frighten you,' it said brightly. 'I thought you would have seen me! Perhaps in your hurry to get shelter you mistook me and my brown garments for part of the tree?'

'I—I—' Nial fought for words, and suddenly realised the man was a monk.

'Ach well,' the voice continued lightly, 'I am so thin that it would be no surprise if you had not noticed me.' The figure stooped in under the branch beside Nial, speaking with the slow precision and soft accents of someone from the West Highlands of Scotland. 'I am Nith, son of Rathan,' said he, squinting upwards as he brushed a quivering droplet of rain from the top edge of his coarsely woven hood. 'But here everyone calls me Cailan, because I am so slight.' He stood a good two inches shorter than Nial, and smelled strongly of wet wool. 'May I ask who you might be? You wear the oddest garment!'

Nial glanced at his bedraggled shorts and thought they were ordinary enough.

'I am Nial.' As he said it, he somehow knew that he had not spoken in English.

Ridiculous. He knew no other language, apart from 'school' French, and it was not that which had come out of his mouth.

He tried again.

'I am Nial!' It sounded the same.

'Do not shout, my friend!' The monk held up a slender, young-looking hand. 'The rain has stopped its noise, or nearly so, and my hood, even when it is as wet as this, is not as thick as it looks!' He reached up and threw it back, and Nial gasped with astonishment to see him shake loose a head of curly blond hair that hung to his shoulders. Cailan looked at him curiously, and cocked his head on one side.

Nial apologised for his wide-eyed stare, and again the strange language formed effortlessly on his tongue. 'But—I thought—monks had their hair short—with a bald bit in the middle? You—you *are* a monk, aren't you?' Still the strange words. Maybe he was going mad.

'Yes, for many months now,' Cailan nodded. 'But you still have not said where you are from. You are not an island man, nor are you a Dane, judging by the way you speak Erse.'

Nial hesitated. Danes? Erse? *Erse!* The ancient Irish language! Now, not only was he suddenly speaking in a tongue that he had never learnt, but he was able to understand it too, for clearly that was what this 'Cailan' was speaking.

'Or,' continued the monk with a slight narrowing of his light blue eyes, 'are the Danes at last teaching their children our way of speech, so that they may in time persecute us even more by sending spies to our Christian sanctuaries?'

'Danes?' said Nial. 'What Danes? Look, I live in Belfast, and I—I—' His voice trailed into silence. What *was* happening? He could make no sense of anything any more; the terrible, freak weather conditions, the strange waterway running where there should be a road with a stone castle hard by it, and worse, this even stranger priest; and now he himself conversing in words that he knew he could not, and yet did, speak and comprehend. His frightened eyes stared at the monk's face.

Cailan's expression changed slowly, from suspicion to curiosity, and then sympathy.

'I do not know of the Bell Fust place, but it has not a Norse ring about it.' He paused. 'Just assure me you are not a Dane.'

'No,' said Nial, his brows furrowed with bewilderment, 'I'm not a Dane.' He was beginning to wonder just what, indeed, he was.

'I am glad of that.' The monk looked pleased. 'Are you by any chance a Christian?'

'Oh, er, yes!' Nial was relieved that they had at least something in common. 'Yes, I am.'

'Well now, that is grand! But wherever did you get such strange things to wear? Come, the rain has stopped at last. Will you come up to Aendrum with me, and tell me about yourself as we go?'

Nial took a deep breath. He had never heard of the place and did not know what to do. The monk took his arm.

'Come.'

'No! That is—oh, please, I don't understand! Who are you? And, well—where am I?' Nial fought back a childish, but very strong desire to burst into tears.

'Ach! Are you lost?' Cailan reached out and took both

Nial's hands in his own. 'That is a dreadful feeling, even for a tall lad like yourself,' said he, and he smiled again, a warm, friendly smile revealing a set of long, even teeth. 'Come then, and have no fear of me; I only fight Danes, and that solely in defence of the church of Saint Mohee. Come up with me, and perhaps Abbot Sedna will know of this Bell Fust place, and can set you on your way.' And he led Nial out into the sunshine that glinted golden on the puddles and shining, rain-soaked grass by the pathway.

'Wait,' said Nial. Everything was so odd, that he desperately wanted to go back and see that *Cuan* still existed. 'My boat. May I first see that she's all right?'

'Why yes! I did not know you had one! Where is it pulled up?'

'Over there.' Nial turned and led back past the ford, trying hard not to run.

It was Cailan who could hardly believe his eyes when they rounded the curving shore-line. There, by now almost clear of the ebbing tide, was a boat the like of which he had never seen.

'It is of wood!' he cried, with astonishment. 'Yet so small! And these bits...' He laid an unbelieving hand on the varnished mahogany of the gunwale. 'How have you made them shine so?'

Now another odd thing happened. When Nial wanted to say 'varnish' he found he could not, not in Erse anyway, and he had to say it in English and it sounded very strange. It was stranger to Cailan.

'I do not know what it is,' he said, 'but it is beautiful.' He turned suddenly. 'You did speak truly to me—you are not a Dane?'

'I told you I'm not! Why do you keep on asking me? Why should I be Danish anyway?'

'The Danes build their longships like this, board overlapping board.' Cailan's voice hardened. 'Who built this boat?'

'I have not the least idea,' said Nial, and rather crossly commenced to tidy up the dripping folds of the sail. 'My father bought her, I don't know who from, and I don't know when or even where she was built, either. Anything else?'

Cailan looked uncertain.

'Your father. Who is he? You said you are Nial, and that is a local enough name, but where is your father from, that he can find boats like this? I must know!' He gripped Nial's elbow.

'He's called John Ross, and I think he was born in Belfast too—and if it's anything to you, *his* father was Angus Ross, and came from Scotland.'

'A Scot?' Cailan let the arm go. 'Why did you not say so? I am Dalriadan myself now, and was born and brought up on an island off the long end of Mull. A small but holy place, called Iona.'

Nial looked up. 'Iona!' He grinned delightedly. 'I've been there! My parents took me just last year in our . . .' But again the word seemed to stick, and required translating in the weird fashion, '. . . "yacht" . . .'

'What is that?' said Cailan, his head canted over sideways again. 'You do say strange things!'

'Oh dear!' Nial wondered how long this was going to go on. 'It's a sort of boat. Bigger than *Cuan*.'

'*Cuan?*'

'This one,' said Nial, pointing to the name on her stern.

'What unusual letters!' exclaimed Cailan. 'But Cuan is the name of the lough here. Why call a boat a lough? Is it especially wet and leaky?'

Nial could not answer, and did not see amusement in the

question. Something else was beginning to form in his mind that at least made partial sense in this chaotic afternoon. The lough had not commonly been called Cuan for centuries. Could it possibly be that—that time had slipped back in some way, carrying him with it? And how far back? ... Oh, how preposterous! And yet; it was a crazy thought certainly, but it would explain things; things like the lack of causeway and castle, if this *was* Mahee Island. He looked again at Cailan, who was peering at the gleaming chrome and metalwork of the outboard motor which he had just discovered in the bottom of the boat. A monk. A long-haired monk. And nearby, again if this *was* Mahee, were the remains of Nendrum Abbey. Looking up through the branches of the thorn tree to which *Cuan*'s painter was tied, Nial found himself gazing over the rounded hilltop at a squat, conical, almost steeple-like spire, surmounting a slender stone tower.

He began to sweat, coldly.

'P-pardon m-my asking; but where did you s-say you would take me?'

'Aendrum, of course. I am sure the Abbot can help you.'

Aendrum ... Nendrum ...

'And what s-saint did you say you defended?'

'Ach, not himself now, but his church here. He was our first Abbot, and died nearly five hundred years ago. In fact just last month we had a memorial service for him.'

'Yes, yes,' Nial was holding firmly onto *Cuan*'s bow. 'But his n-name, what was his name?'

'Mohee. Saint Mohee. Why, the island bears it to this d ... Are you all right?'

Nial thought he was going to be sick, saw Cailan rush round the boat towards him, saw the seaweed rise up and hit him hard in the face.

2

Nial, Son of Ross

In his dream, Nial saw the roof of a small African hut over his head, its poles rising up from low walls and meeting in a point at the top, where thatch of some kind showed dimly between them. The only light entered through a tiny doorway, and outside, the natives were chanting softly. A bee bumbled swervingly in through the open space, circled his head, and buzzed out again. He shifted uncomfortably on the prickly blanket, and it rustled as though spread over some kind of reeds or hay ...

Nial sat bolt upright. He was naked. But for his wristwatch he hadn't a stitch of clothing.

He looked again round the native hut. It was no dream. The circle enclosed by the rough stone wall was not much more than six or seven feet in diameter, and as bare as the hard clay floor. There was no furniture of any kind other than the 'bed' in the curve of the wall, and no sign whatever of his clothes.

He got to his feet and cautiously stood up, stepping into the centre where the headroom was greatest. A breath of sun-warmed air from the door wafted round his body, and he stooped to peer out—and found his view at once obstructed. Someone outside ducked down and entered, then stepped to one side, letting in more light. And all at once Nial recognised the thin, straight-nosed, youngish face, the brown robes and the long fair hair; everything came back to him in a rush.

Cailan smiled.

'Ach, that is grand! You had us all worried. Are you all right now?' He put a small white bundle down on the bed. 'Your garment is still very damp, so put this on for the moment. We have missed Prayers, but they will soon be finished and we can go and see the Abbot.'

It was all very well for the monk to be so calm and practical; but for Nial, finding himself cut off from people and surroundings that he knew, and pitched willy-nilly into—could it really be?—a different time and period, and among monks at that, the strain was considerable.

Cailan saw the question in the brown eyes, and cocked his head on one side, just as he had before when they were under the tree.

'What is it?'

'I—I don't know—' Nial struggled to clear his thoughts. 'That is—well, you don't realise, but I—' and suddenly it burst from him in a torrent, 'I'm not here really; I can't be! Not if this is Nendrum Abbey and you're a monk of it, because it's not here now—at least in my time, and . . .'

'Wait a bit!' Cailan sat on the bed and lifted aside the bundle. 'Sit here by me and tell me—slowly.'

Nial lowered himself onto the coarse blanket, and taking the white cloth from the monk's slender hands (which felt real enough when he touched them), he shook it out in front of himself, and stared unseeingly at what seemed to be a simple, whitish tunic with holes for arms and head. He let it fall onto his lap, and turned to Cailan.

'Look. Something—I don't know what or how—has happened to me. All I know is that I *think*, unless this is some sort of hoax or I've gone mad, that I come from a different time—different age—oh, how *can* I explain when I don't understand it myself?' The clear blue eyes stared, unmoving, into his own. Then he had an idea. 'What year is this?'

The answer came crisply and pat: 'Nine-seventy-four.'

Nial put a hand to his forehead. His heart weighed like lead in his chest. 'I was born in the middle of the twentieth century.'

Cailan's blue eyes opened wide, narrowed incredulously, and then widened again.

'That,' he said slowly, 'has not—happened—yet.'

'Exactly.' Nial gazed down at the tunic. He raised it again. 'Does this thing have a right way round?'

'What? Ach, yes. The embroidery just below the neck goes to the front.' He helped pull it over Nial's head, and then rummaged in the straw under the blanket. 'You had better have my spare belt and shoes.'

Nial wrapped the strange woven-wool strip round his middle, and tied it with a half-bow. The shoes were plain pieces of cow-skin, complete with hair, which when Cailan had shown him how to lace them on with the leather thongs, were rather too small and yet looked like overgrown bedroom slippers. He stood up and straightened the tunic. It reached to just above his knees.

Cailan rose beside him in the tapering space. 'Your name is Nial, you said. Can what you tell me be true?'

'How should *I* know? Except that there should have been a castle and a causeway where I left the boat—and there wasn't. And you thought my—my "shorts"—were funny—' The word had needed 'translating' into English.

'Your what?'

' "Shorts"—"trousers"—what I was wearing. You see? You don't even know what I'm talking about. Look.' He thrust out his left wrist so that the shining stainless steel wristwatch was about a foot from Cailan's puzzled eyes. 'Ever seen one of these?'

Cailan gazed at the slowly revolving second hand and reared back, striking his head with some force against a roof pole. 'It—it is living.'

'You haven't, have you! Well, it's a "watch"; an ordinary, everyday "watch" for telling the time.'

'The time? It—it certainly is beautiful! Does it hurt when it goes round like that?'

'No, of course not. Look. Things like it and, er—"television" and "cars" and "aeroplanes" and "submarines" and "trains", are all commonplace to me. I bet you haven't heard of one of them. Well? Have you?'

'No. Not one. I admit it.' A bell jangled briefly outside. Cailan cleared his throat noisily. 'Come. I really think we had better go and see the Abbot.'

'Wait,' said Nial, again. 'Another thing. If I go out of this hut and find myself in a monastery full of buildings and people and churches and things, instead of a few piles of stone, bare foundations and a wall or two, then there'll be no doubt about it—time slipping, I mean. None at all. You did say this was Island Mahee, didn't you?'

Cailan was looking very serious, and rather blank. 'Indeed I did,' he said quietly. 'I had better go out first. You will excuse me. You are going to have a shock, my friend.'

Now Nial had few doubts that his guess about buildings and people was right, but what he saw when he straightened up outside the doorway of the hut made him gasp and clutch at the brown cloth bunched over Cailan's arm. About twenty feet in front of him a bare stone wall surmounted by another apparently built up with sods of earth, curved away in both directions. Over the top of it peeped a number of thatched roofs, some round and some long. Beyond them was a long shingled roof with odd-looking knobs sticking up at each end, and to the right of it the great narrow tapering column of the round, stone tower dominated the entire scene. The thing must be something like sixty feet tall, thought Nial.

'Come,' Cailan took his hand as though he were a child. 'We must go this way. All visitors have to have their names written in our book.' He led off to the left where there was a narrow gap between the great curved wall and a lower one running at right-angles to it. Nial looked back, and to his astonishment saw that the hut next to Cailan's was made completely of stone, roof and all, and shaped like a gigantic bee-hive. There were others of wood and stone mixed, just beyond it.

'Come on,' Cailan grinned at him. 'You can study everything later. I can hardly wait until Dima sees you! He keeps the book and is very interested in people. And you, let us face it, would seem to be rather special!'

Nial followed through the gap, feeling somehow undressed as he walked along in the short tunic. Now more buildings appeared on his left, and ahead on what looked like a narrow terrace, from the edge of which the ground sloped steeply away among trees.

'Through here—' Cailan led to the right into a narrow slit which slanted diagonally and unexpectedly into the curved wall. There was not room to go through two abreast, though it widened out in a few feet to where a man dressed much like Cailan but wearing a long auburn beard sat whittling at a piece of wood. He looked up and stared at Nial, but Cailan led on through a doorway under a rounded wooden arch on the right.

Inside, Nial found himself in a roughly rectangular enclosure surrounded by lean-to sheds, rather like market stalls. Ahead was a small wooden building with three little slit-like windows alone breaking the plain planking of the near wall.

'Dima!' Cailan looked round, and then nudged Nial and nodded in the direction of one of the lean-tos. On a pile of straw lay a round little man in brown robes, fast asleep in the sun. 'It was market day yesterday, and his turn on bell duty last night. One moment.' He strode over, and with a toe gently prodded the sleeper, and once more, but in an exaggeratedly deep voice, said, 'Brother Dima!'

The figure leapt and thrashed, with straw flying in all directions, and in a high-pitched voice mumbled, 'Yesh, my Abbot, I—I—Oh! Oh, Cailan! How could you!'

'Customer,' grinned Cailan, motioning Nial forward. 'Nial, Son of Ross, and not ordinary.'

'I will get the book—Not ordinary? Why not?' The little man peered at Nial short-sightedly. 'He looks normal to me. Bit tall, though. Hello! Welcome to Aendrum!' And he trotted off round the corner of the wooden building and returned almost at once with a quill pen dripping pale blue ink, and 'the book'.

Nial's eyes widened when he saw it. The cover of 'the book' was of wood, and decorated all over with designs burnt on with a hot needle; spirals, twists, and diamond patterns; and the pages were thick yellow parchment, apparently covered, where they were not actually written on, with what looked very like 'doodles.'

Dima's face crinkled up in a toothless smile.

'My book,' he said. 'I should not be proud of it, but I am, and do many a pennansh as a result.' And carefully placing his tongue between his gums, he began to scratch Nial's name under a very complicated drawing of some kind of animal.

Cailan was right. Dima was very interested in people, and for all his lack of teeth could winkle information from them right briskly, so that although Cailan had not meant to tell him of Nial's past, or rather 'future', when they left the quadrangle a little later and went through a gate by the end of the building, Dima was down on his knees on the paving stones, mumbling prayers for all he was worth. It bothered Nial, but not Cailan, who led him now beside a high wooden fence in front of some thatched huts. It was these roofs he had earlier seen from the other side of the curved wall which now bent in towards them. A narrow gateway interrupted it, and leaning against the earthen battlement on top of it, stood another bearded guard. He nodded at Cailan as they passed by, not going through the gate, but turning hard left round the end of the fence into another part of the enclosure. And there, tapering into the sky above them, was the round tower.

Beyond it stood a small church; a long structure with narrow, round-topped windows piercing its side walls, and only a doorway in the near gable. But that gable was fantastic. To begin with, it was recessed back about a foot or so into the building and had been plastered and seemingly whitewashed. This entire white area was completely covered with the most elaborate designs, just like Dima's 'book', only more so. In fact the detail was so utterly and minutely involved that it was impossible to make any sense of any of the patterns from where Nial now stood at the foot of the huge stone tower.

The latter had a narrow plinth projecting round its base at a convenient height from the ground, and against this were sitting two broad, well-built monks, who wore very dark robes and were almost identical to look at. When Cailan spoke, they replied with strong accents, looked at Nial, and shook their heads.

'Is all right,' said one of them, standing up and throwing back his hood to reveal a mass of wavy black hair. He offered his hand to Nial. Nial put his out, and found not it, but the wrist, being shaken. 'Is all right, I yust tell Cailan here you is no a Dane. I know, because I one. That surprise you? Ah, but is Christian one! No fighting battles any more! Here my brother, Ranvaig.' Nial nodded politely to the other, and wondered, since Cailan was obviously in such fear of 'the Danes', what these two were doing as monks in an Irish monastery. It occured to him then that by 'Danes', Cailan probably meant Vikings, but he couldn't remember enough from his history classes to know if this was a Viking period or not.

Up the side of the tower facing the church, Cailan now showed him a ladder which extended to a height of about nine or ten feet, where a rather odd, tapering doorway was built into the wall. The ladder wobbled a lot as Nial followed up it.

Inside the door was a wooden-floored room much like the interior of Cailan's hut, and also barely six feet in diameter. But in place of a bed, though none the less carefully fitted to the curve of the wall, was a small table with straight legs carved again with intricate, twisted designs. And seated at the table was a short, thin, bald-headed man dressed entirely in white.

Prime Abbot Sedna O'Deman rose to his bare feet and bowed with a gently inclined head. Cailan returned the bow.

'My Abbot, this is Nial, Son of Ross, and he is rather peculiar.'

'Brother Cailan!' said the Abbot in a slow, deep voice. 'How often need I tell you to beware of your speech? You will embarrass the boy! If you mean he is not from our island, I can see that. Son of Ross, I am happy to . . .'

'You do not understand, Abbot. Nial is not of our time.'

The Abbot looked at Cailan sharply. 'This is not another of your jokes, is it? I know I like happiness in Aendrum, but sometimes you over-do that aspect.'

'I am serious, Abbot,' Cailan bowed his head, and then fixed his eyes steadily on the old man's face. 'If what he says can be true, and we know of many miracles—well, Nial has told me that he does not expect to be born for almost a thousand years.'

Abbot Sedna stared back at Cailan without moving, for fully ten seconds. Then he slowly shifted his gaze to Nial. 'This is so?'

'Yes, er—Abbot.'

'Oh? You *are* Christian, my son?'

'Yes, a "Presbyterian".' He fought for the word. 'At least, my parents are.'

'I have not heard of that, but as a believer in Christ, you are welcome to my house. Have you been offered food?'

'I've had lunch quite recently, thank you,' said Nial, without thinking.

'If you want; ask. What we have is yours.' The Abbot smiled, and sat down again on the three-legged stool. He glanced sideways at Nial. 'What story have you been telling my susceptible Cailan?'

It was very hard indeed to explain the whole thing again, and the old man had not heard of Belfast. However, prompted by Cailan, Nial ended up showing the Abbot his watch.

'Great goodness!' The bald head jerked forwards as the Abbot's eyes noticed the long second hand flicking round the dial. 'What an extraordinary thing! You say it tells the time? Well, well! I wonder how you make it turn like that? Our sun clock by the cell outside does the same thing, though only the shadow moves. Did you not see it? Cailan will show you. It is very good at time-telling.'

'But not on a cloudy day, surely?' The words were out before Nial could check them.

The Abbot made a little bow, and came up with a wry and very comical look on his thin face. His deep voice purred.

'That is very, very true, my son. And now, Cailan,' he continued, 'take the boy round our establishment and give him everything he needs. A cloak, for instance. I hear Brothers Ranvaig and Shetelig are very pleased with their new dark ones. You could start by taking him up the Bell House, and pointing out everything from the top.' He paused and then turned to Nial. 'I was expecting something of this sort to happen,' he said. 'Our founder, Mohee, died in the year 497. This being 974, something was bound to happen. Quite obviously, you must be—er—it. You will doubtless tell us your message when you are ready; in the meantime we are honoured to have you among us.'

'Message?' Nial was already somewhat muddled by the whole situation, but at this his face really lengthened in surprise. 'I have no message! Look I had no idea this was going to happen —it's as much of a mystery to me as it is to you!'

'Apparently more so, my son.' The Abbot's eyes sparkled. 'Do not worry! You must have been sent for a purpose. If you do not know what that is, it will be shown to you before long. And now I must study this work before Evening Worship.' He indicated what looked like a short piece of board, lying on the table. 'Excuse me.'

Cailan tugged at Nial's elbow and pointed upwards. There was a long vertical plank fixed to the wall, its top disappearing through a hole in the high ceiling. It was pierced every eighteen inches or so with semi-circular holes, and using these as hand- and footholds, the young monk started to climb.

Nial found it rather easier than a ladder provided you started with the right foot, for the holes were offset to left and right. The thing ran the full height of the tower, and Nial's arms were aching before he reached the top. Altogether there were five floors including the one they came in on, and whereas that one had a space of some twelve feet between floor and ceiling, all the rest had much less headroom. Cailan rather breathlessly explained that this was so that they could pull the outside ladder up into the first room and close the door in the event of an attack.

Each room was roughly the same in diameter, and the glassless windows were few but draughtily large, and curiously positioned between the floors so that one window lit two storeys. One floor had a straw bed and a sort of delicate tripod thing standing on its own beside it, the others seemed to be mainly used for storage.

At the top they were greeted by an elderly monk called Aengus, who showed no sign of emotion at all when Cailan told him Nial's story, but instead smiled at him with the piercing eyes of a seaman, and reaching into a wooden box on the floor, withdrew a strange, tall and tapering object of a lightish fawn-green colour.

'If that is true,' he said lightly, 'you should see this.'

The thing had a looped handle at its narrower end, and Nial took it carefully, for it was obviously heavy. And then he saw it was a bell, rather like a long version of those worn by the Swiss cows he had once seen in a magazine somewhere. But it was indeed immensely heavy for its size, having been apparently dipped at some stage into molten bronze which had dried in dribblets and bumps on its iron surface.

Aengus kept a hand on the clapper, a totally separate and unattached little rod of bronze.

'One chime out of it, and everyone would start going to Evening Prayers, which should not happen for a while yet. Do you like it?'

It was by no means beautiful to Nial's eyes, but was clearly considered special.

'It is a fine bell indeed. Is it very old?'

'Old?' The glittering eyes crinkled at their edges. 'Bless you, yes! Yes, it is—well, let me see—five hundred and er, forty-two years is it not, Brother?'

'Yes. You see, Nial,' Cailan reverently took the bell from him and returned it to its box, 'it was given to Saint Mohee by none other than Patric himself, before ever the monastery here was founded.'

'*Saint* Patrick? Goodness!' Nial stared at them. 'And you let me handle it?'

The old monk looked steadily at the youth. 'Who better? I can hear what is said in the Abbot's room from up here. You are probably the first to have been especially sent to us by God since that time.'

'Oh, now look here!' exclaimed Nial, thoroughly embarrassed. 'I've had enough of this! Even if time has slipped in some way, I'm not an angel or a saint, or anything like that. I'm not even a particularly regular church-goer, except at school where you have to. Believe me, I'm quite ordinary, and certainly was not "sent" . . .' Cailan was looking at him, head tilted and eyebrows raised . . . 'at least, I don't think so. Really, I don't!'

'Ach, we shall see, Nial. As Abbot Sedna told you, this will become apparent in due course. And now, look,' and he pointed out of the southernmost window of the four that lit the space, 'let me show you the layout here. We are the oldest and biggest monastery in Ulaidh (he pronounced it "Ulli"), you know; there is much to see . . .'

'Ulli?'

'Yes—ach! I was forgetting! This part of our country is called that, and to the north and over the Straights of Moyle is the kingdom of Dalriada. What name do you know it by?'

'Ulster, here.' Nial felt very queer, almost as though he *was* something special. 'But I have heard of the Straights of Moyle, and the other place. Now—that is, well—I know them simply as the "North Channel" and "Scotland".'

'Ulster—Ulli; well, well! And "Scotland". That is to the point, anyway. Oh, by the way, Aengus,' Cailan turned to the old monk, 'he tells me his father's father came from this "Scotland" and, believe it or not, had the same name as yourself! Or do I mean "will have"? How very odd!'

'That's the church, isn't it?' Nial was leaning out of the window and staring down at the long narrow building with the steeply pitched roof. Cailan bent over his shoulder.

'Aye. It is rather special in shape, and quite new, like this Bell House. One of our Brothers went on a Mission away twice across the sea to the land in the south, where there is a monastery started by another of our people a long time ago. We tried to make a church like the one he saw there. He said it should be much wider, only we cannot think how to roof such a space safely without cluttering the inside with a lot of posts. However, we *can* just get everyone in at once; though if we do, there is not room to kneel comfortably. Look, just below us here, the small wood-roofed building is one of the old oratories; the other remaining one, over there to the right beyond the church, is on the very spot occupied by Saint Mohee's first one, and the wooden cross in front of it is a replica of that which he himself raised, though Ailil has carved it a lot.'

Nial saw what looked like a pile of stones just a few yards from the door of the main church, and asked what they were going to build there.

'Build? Why, bless you, it *is* built! That is a stone cell; the very reason we sited our big church just here! It is the cell of Mohee!'

A roughly paved pathway, curving past an upright slab of stone that Nial presumed was the sundial, led round the cell from the church door, and then turned away south to follow the sweep of the stone wall which he now realised he had seen before. That had been the day his parents had shown him over the ruins of the site. How strange it seemed! It had then been a crumbled misery in comparison to what he now saw, its earthen parapet obviously proclaiming it as part of a defence system. The path departed briefly from it to bend, in deference it seemed, towards the huge wooden cross, and then continued round to a gateway, guarded again by a bearded brown figure holding a spear.

'Why do some of you have beards, and some not?'

'Ach well, those that do are our helpers. They act as guards mostly, or are in charge of some of the animals; but mainly they guard the cashels.'

'Cashels?'

'Aye, the big walls. Look, there are three of them, see? Curving round in circles, one outside the other. Not very round, I admit, but that is because they are very old, and have once or twice fallen out in places, and been rebuilt. The middle one to the west of us here even stands inside its original foundations, I hear. Many the attack they have stood, too. Some successful at that, I believe, but not recently, of course. Here, inside the inner cashel, apart from the Bell House and church and place where you met Dima, those round, thatched wooden huts are all big cells for the senior Brothers. Then outside, in the area bounded by the middle cashel there are the workshops.' He pointed to one in the southwest that was producing clouds of blue smoke. 'That is the iron foundry—Critan looks as if he is having the usual bother getting his fire hot enough for the melting. The next building this way is the store that Critan uses as his cell along with his boy helper and the carpenter, who works in the completely round hut next to it. Between that and next again you will find a gate to that path which goes right down the hill through the outer cashel to the shore. The tide runs strongly there, and that is where we do our ablutions—for your future information.'

'Thanks,' said Nial, thinking that he would make that his next visit. It had been a long time since his ramble on Wood Island. Looking through the west window, he could see the isle itself—and it was, to his astonishment, practically covered with trees, which it most certainly hadn't been that morning.

'On this side of the gate,' continued Cailan, unaware of his thoughts, 'Aed does near miracles with bronze—look, this is one of his brooches—. He showed Nial the pin that held his cloak together at his chest. It was long and finely decorated. One end curled round a bronze ring of just over an inch in diameter. This had a gap in it, so that after piercing the material, one could push the pin through and then 'lock it' in place by rotating the ring. The flattened ends of the latter were delicately worked with a small spiral design.

'It's lovely, Cailan!'

'Yes, and it was nice of him; he gave it me on our Saint's Day last month. Anyway, that is where he works. By the hut is his cell, which he shares with our cook and his boys. The

Cooking House is next, the long narrow roof, there. Your "short" did you call it? Well, it and your shoes are there now, unless Ronan has dropped them on the fire in his efforts to dry them! Then there is the School, and the Eating House where . . .'

'School?'

'Why yes—but it is famous! Not that you would know—unless—'

Nial began to feel awkward. He knew perfectly well what thought had entered Cailan's mind, and he had no desire to mention again that the site would end up as a heap of overgrown ruins. He turned and stared miserably out from the height of the north window. The breeze blew freshly across his face.

In the other directions the views over the surroundings had been widespread. He had seen the entire island, a lot of which stretched away to the east of the monastery, divided from it by a deeply dug ditch beyond the outer cashel and only connected by a stone causeway running for a short distance parallel to the shore. Away beyond, he had been able to see from end to end of the lough he knew as Strangford.

To the south, beyond the little narrows through which he had so happily sailed *Cuan* that morning (though it seemed years ago), lay the open waters and the rounded green hillocks of the various islands. But what had inevitably struck him, and disturbed him, was the complete absence of not only his parents' boat, but of the entire fleet of yachts normally anchored off Whitecrock. There was an utter lack of any buildings there that he could see, of the castle ruins, or even the castle that he knew should stand on this side of Sketrick Island, beyond Rainey. And never a house or a bungalow anywhere in sight. It could not be a dream.

And now, looking down to the north, he could see a strip of fast-drying mud between Mahee and Reagh, crossed only by a pile of gravelly stones, instead of the metalled roadway. At least he could see *Cuan*'s stern peeping out from behind a thorn tree down there. She was real!

But on raising his gaze over the wooded hills beyond the shining mud of Reagh Bay he saw something that made his heart dance with relief: standing up proud and blue in the distance were the solid and unmistakable outlines of Cave Hill, Divis, and the Black Mountain. It was these that he saw rising over the city when in the morning he threw back the bedroom curtains of his Belfast home.

'Cailan! Cailan, look! There! Those mountains—that's where I live! Belfast's just at the foot of them, between them and us. That's where my home . . .' He paused, the quick joy as suddenly gone from his face. 'That's where—my home—will be. Oh, Cailan.'

The two monks looked at his young, deeply distressed face. Cailan reached forward and gently took Nial's hands into his own.

'I know. I think I understand. It must be hard indeed to bear. But it will be for the good, you will see. Have faith, Nial. God will return you safely, as soon as your Purpose is fulfilled.'

'But I tell you, I haven't got a "purpose"! I haven't got a message or anything!'

'You have life, Nial.' Cailan looked him straight in the eyes, and then suddenly nudged him, and grinned. 'Are we such bad company?'

The tension at least partly broke, and Nial could not help but smile back.

'No, of course not!'

'Well then, say goodbye to Aengus now, and come on

down to interrupt the Abbot and tell him that we have found Bell Fust.'

The Abbot listened, and to Nial's relief, began to nod.
'I think I have it,' droned the deep voice. 'Cailan is wrong; it is not "Fust", you say, but "Fast", and the first word could be the same as our "Mouth". There are two rivers there, one great and the other small. I remember drinking from the latter once, and it is called the Farset. The land is fearfully swampy, but there were a few dwellings about. Should a town grow there, it might well be called "Mouth of the Farset".' What he actually said sounded like 'Bee-ull na Farset'. Nial thanked him, thanked him very much, and followed Cailan out down the ladder into the warm sunshine.

He felt at least a bit happier now, and almost enjoyed the sound of voices and birds, and the mooing of the cows he had seen from the tower, drinking at a large round pond just inside the outer cashel, beyond the school building.

The sun was beautifully hot, the sky clear, and he walked lightly and easily in the unrestricting tunic as Cailan led the way through the near gateway and out into the second enclosure. Several brown-clad figures were grouped around, the Danish twins among them, and they made way for Nial, and smiled and welcomed him, so that he felt warm inside, too.

In the dark Cooking House it was stifling. He was not surprised to find that the big, jolly, heavily-built cook, Ronan, and one of his two boy helpers were dressed solely in belted tunics like his own. The younger boy, aged about eleven, Nial thought, wore a long cloak of coarse material but nothing else. In his hand was Nial's folded clasp knife. They and several of the monks were standing round an open fireplace from which the smoke eddied and swirled round the building, finally to find its way through a gaping hole in the roof. One of them had Nial's shorts in his hands, while another was showing a gym-shoe to the elder boy.

Ronan, sweat glistening on his podgy face, came bustling forward, rubbing his hands together.

'Ah, Cailan!' His voice was very high-pitched, almost falsetto. 'So this is the miraculous owner of these wonderful things! Welcome to you, my son, welcome! But alas, for all the heat, the garment is not quite dry! Well, you see, it is so unusual and the material so even and finely worked, that we, er, we keep having to show it to everyone, and that means taking it down from the line there, so—but the shoes are dry, yes, oh, what wonderful shoes! Here, ah, thank you Brother, here they are, my son. Oh dear, I am overcome, that is, *we* are, with curiosity. Please will you stay and tell us what in the world this white substance is?' He tapped the rubber sole of the shoe. 'We have none of us seen anything like it. And please, what *is* that?' He pointed to the lad holding the stainless steel sailing knife. It was clear that not one of them had recognised its purpose, and when the boy came nervously forward, Nial showed him how to open out the blade. The look of astonishment on the youngster's face was matched in an instant by each of his elders. There was a gasp, a second's silence, and then a burst of questions.

'But how do you make iron shine like that?' 'Is it silver?' 'Who makes such things?' 'How did you get it so sharp?' Someone held up a bleeding finger, and the knife passed (more carefully) from hand to amazed hand.

Cailan lifted his voice.

'All in good time, Brothers! Give our guest a chance, now! And give him his wonderful knife back. There. It is nearly time for Evening Worship, and before that I have to wheedle a cloak for him out of Cathal. Nial, will you eat with us after Prayers, and then honour us at the fireplace with a few answers? There is so much, so very much you could tell us.'

It was obvious that sooner or later they were going to find out about the future of their establishment, but perhaps the blow would fall softer on well-filled stomachs. Nial bent to unlace the cowhide slippers.

'Of course I will. Besides, there's quite a lot that you can tell me! Now, do you mind if I put my own shoes on? I'm afraid my feet are not as hard as yours, and these things chafe a bit!'

The visit to Cathal, who lived in one of the wooden huts in the enclosure behind the Bell House, did indeed take a long time, because at first he could not be found. It appeared that he was also the community's keenest bee-keeper, and whenever a swarm happened, which was surprisingly often, he would be called upon to deal with it. Eventually he arrived, a few rather stupefied bees still clinging to his robes and buzzing off for brief trips round his head. He apologised profusely to Nial.

'Quite unforgivable! Most sorry! Swarm, you know. Had to cope. They never sting me, though they have a go at most of us from time to time. Oh! Should have seen the fun when they swarmed in the church door once. Abbot and everyone, all trapped! Danes could have walked in, you know. No one to stop them! Never sting me, though . . .'

'A cloak, Cathal, please.'

'What? Ah! Oh! For the lad? Of course! Stupid. Yes, well . . .'

'The Abbot suggested one of the new dark ones, like you gave to the twins.'

'The very thing! Most soft, those turned out. *Wish* I could remember what it was I added to the dye of that batch! Made quite a difference. Ah! Here we are! Thought there was one left—and a big one too. Just about right for a tall lad like you.' He reached up and draped it round Nial's shoulders, then paused. 'Where is your pin, my son?'

'I'm afraid I haven't got one. You see I . . .'

'Never be bothered! Tie a knot in it. A lot of us do, you know. Not everyone gets given things like Cailan here. There! Lovely! Now, what about a nice pair of—goodness! What remarkable footwear! Quite remarkable—Go 'way bee! —Quite remark . . .'

'If you want to know more about them,' Cailan took Nial firmly by the arm and steered him through the low door, 'wait until after supper.'

Once outside, he grinned.

'There is *one* who has not yet discovered about you, it would seem.'

'Very refreshing,' said Nial, for he had found all the attention embarrassing. 'That reminds me, Cailan. I wouldn't mind a wash.'

'Wash? What f . . . Ach, I see what you mean. This way then. There is just time.'

Climbing back up the steeply sloping path from the water's edge, they could hear old Aengus clanging away on the Saint's Bell at the top of the round tower.

'He holds it up in each window in turn, so that it may be heard on all sides,' said Cailan, leading through the extremely narrow gap between the walls and the prickly thatch of two huts. By the doorway of one of these, a short burly man was pinning on his hooded cloak. Cailan halted.

'Ach, Aed! Nial, this is the man who helped me to. . . .'

'I hope you feel better now,' interrupted the monk, hitching his hood up over his head and peering out at Nial. 'I hear you are going to tell us something of the future, tonight. That should be good for us! The past is rather boring in the face of Prophecy. Are you coming to Prayers?'

'If I may.'

'Good, then we can walk together. Cailan has told you of our little procession? We always do this morning and evening. I like a bit of ceremony, myself. Do you speak Latin?'

'Heavens, no! At least—I don't think so.' Nial, who normally had but a very few words of prep-school Latin, such as 'sagittas' and the declension of 'amo', could not now be sure.

'A most useful tongue, I assure you,' said Aed. 'Besides, it sings well. Ah, here comes Ronan. We follow him. Ready?'

In single file, and with Nial feeling self-conscious under his hood at being so high up ahead of the other lay-folk, the procession moved off towards the south gate of the inner cashel. The flagged pathway was uneven, and required a watchful eye if toe-stubbing was to be avoided, so there was no difficulty in keeping one's head reverently bowed. On passing through the gate, the leading monks broke into a lilting song and followed the paving round to the left, keeping close to the wall. The first verse of the tune was merely hummed, a wavering, nasal melody that seemed right in the open air on that rounded drumlin. When the words came, they were indeed in Latin, and the chant rose and fell with them in a weird and slightly disjointed form. The deep voices somehow blended with the rough grey stonework that surrounded them.

Further along to his left, against the setting sun, Nial could see the thatch of the school over the cashel rampart, and he found himself wondering what was taught there. As the path swung round the upstanding slab of the curious sundial, and led them, still singing, in under the pale, profusely decorated gable of the little church, he realised at least one school subject must be art.

Inside the church, the walls were hung with linen draperies embroidered with Bible scenes, weird twisted animals, entwined and intertwined with 'knotwork' patterns, so that there was colour and light everywhere, despite the tiny unglazed windows. Small, smoking and guttering lamps were suspended from the dark beams of the roof.

Arranged longitudinally were plain wooden benches, and as Nial took his place beside Cailan, about half-way along on the right, he saw that even these were covered in a mass of lightly carved designs and scenes. The floor was flagged with what were obviously the stone tops of graves, and at the eastern end was a rough altar of uncut boulders, on which, by complete contrast, there was no decoration whatever other than a small, plain, wooden cross.

Now the voices sounded louder and different, filling the enclosed space with life and sound and happiness. Even the words of the hymn's last verse were sung out with joy in every throat, and with a lifting, final note, the tune seemed to soar into the roof-space and hang there indefinitely.

Nial found himself quite unable to follow the service, but among all the kneeling and standing and sitting that went on, he recognised the often mentioned names of Patric, Mohee, and Aendrum.

He was suddenly conscious of everyone looking in his

direction, and in the midst of all the Latin, he heard his name spoken. He plucked at Cailan's robe.

'What's he saying?' he hissed.

'Just welcoming you—as a prophet—and messenger—'

'I'm neither!'

'Shhh! Do not be silly, my friend, you must be. Hush now, he is starting the Benediction.'

3
'What is Steel?'

The dusk was closing in as everyone trooped round to the Eating House. Spluttering and rather strong-smelling little wick lamps hung from the rafters, casting wavering pear-shaped areas of shadow over the long tables and benches there. The meal was interesting, for it consisted mainly of fruit in the form of apples, and various berries. There were two kinds of cheese, both crumbly, and a heavy sort of wholemeal bread served with butter which tasted slightly rancid, though no one seemed to mind. In front of each diner, an oval hole was cut in the oak table-top in which rested a hollowed cow-horn filled with a sweet, somehow 'scenty' tasting drink. This, if the swaying sensation in Nial's head afterwards was anything to go by, was distinctly alcoholic.

The Abbot, seated at the end of the table beside him, to begin with did his best to keep his questions until the meal was finished. Everyone had produced short knives by way of table-cutlery, and when Nial duly opened his sailing knife for the same purpose, the Abbot's eyes opened very wide indeed. He paused in mid-bite, coughed, and blinked. It was too much for him.

'My son, I, er—I was delighted to hear you are to speak to us after we have finished eating, and I know you will tell us much then, but—er, well, I—I have never seen such a knife in my life! What—er, that is, perhaps you would be good enough —er—to mention it in your talk?'

'Of course. But I don't mind telling you while I eat, if you'd prefer it.'

'No, no, my son—no, you eat up. No, we can wait, we can wait. My! It does look sharp!'

'It's "steel".' Nial found himself 'translating' again.

' "Steel"? What sort of metal—no. No, you eat up; we must not spoil your meal.' And the Abbot busied himself with a hunk of bread, his own rust-stained knife leaving parallel scores and ridges on the bright yellow butter as he spread it. He stopped, peered at the iron implement and back at Nial's shining blade, and then at the smooth surface of the butter on Nial's bread. Then he straightened up and sighed deeply.

'I shall do three hours of penance tonight for the envious thoughts that at this moment fill my head!' And he crossed himself and somewhat lethargically continued eating. Nial managed, but only just, to keep his face straight.

At last he declared he could eat no more, and at once there was a murmur of excitement. With almost a single movement the monks wiped their knives on the palms of their hands and looked expectantly up to the end of the table. The Abbot rose to his feet with a great clearing of his throat, and everyone got up and stepped back over the benches to stand with bowed heads as he made a little thanksgiving prayer.

The activity that followed was instant. Tables were pushed back against the walls, benches were rearranged round the great open fireplace in the middle of the floor, and the fire was poked up into a blaze. The Abbot's chair, a massive throne carved all over with intertwined beasts, was manoeuvred into position by it. A stool with three legs was placed on the right of the chair and Nial was led to it by Cailan, who rather proudly settled himself on the floor at his feet. Everyone sat down. There was an awkward silence, and then the Abbot spoke in deep, but loud and sing-song tones.

'My Brothers, by now all of you must know of the great miracle that God has seen fit to bestow upon us. Our young friend here is most special. He has convinced me that he has effected, and apparently not through any wish of his own, a journey *back* in time—er—from the future.' He hesitated, as though puzzled by his own words.

'It is clear that he has some great message for us, though in the mystery of God's ways, he tells me it has not yet been revealed to him just what that message might be. It is certain however, that some wonderful thing is about to happen; and for the benefit of us, or perhaps of our memory and that of the Christian work of Aendrum Abbey, this young man has been sent.' And then he dropped his voice and began to chat quite normally.

'And now, Nial, my son, *I* shall ask the first question, for once my good Brothers start, my feeble voice is likely to be drowned! And, oh dear me, I *must* know more about that marvellous knife of yours! You said it was made of "steel", or something?'

Nial shifted nervously on the stool, but felt glad his first question should not be about the Abbey's future.

'Y-yes, Abbot. It is "steel", and I think I'm right in saying that that is a form of very good iron. It retains a sharp edge better than ordinary iron, I know, and this particular type of "steel" that my knife is made of doesn't rust either.'

A monk seated on one of the benches raised a hand.

'My Abbot, may I ask more about this "steel"?'

'Ah, Critan! You with your knowledge of iron-making are bound to be interested in this! Please go on.'

The monk turned to Nial, the firelight glowing on the keen-eyed, reddish face.

'Perhaps you could show me how this metal is made? I have good iron-rock at the moment, and such a hard and rustless thing would be of immense use to us.'

Nial felt dismayed and inadequate, for he would have loved to be able to help.

'I'm awfully sorry, but I know nothing of its manufacture at all. I *think* there is some "carbon" mixed in, but I'm not sure.'

' "Carbon"?'

'Yes, you know—like "charcoal"—er, part-burnt wood.' The words came easier.

'Ah, yes! We have lots of that.'

'But I think also that it needs a very great heat indeed,' Nial added, doubtfully.

'Oh. Well, come and see me tomorrow and . . .'

'Pardon me, my Abbot!' It was Cathal, the bee-keeper. 'Pardon me, but his shoes! See? Oh, *strange* things! Saw them when I gave him his cloak. Fascinated! Please could he tell us of them?'

The Abbot nodded, and Nial held out a foot and gazed at the blue and white gym-shoe, and began to think what an awful lot twentieth-century folk like himself took utterly for granted.

It was quite a business trying to explain about rubber, though the cloth 'uppers' were understood easily enough, as were the brass-rimmed lace-holes. Then there were more questions about his shorts, and as he wasn't wearing them, they were brought from the Cooking House and handed round so that everyone could try doing up and undoing the zips, and admire the neatness of the machine-stitching. Of course Nial did not say it was done by machine, because fortunately he realised just in time that he would never manage to describe such things even if he did know how they worked. The zips, made of transparent red plastic, he just had to explain, and said it was like glass only more flexible, but since every window he had seen there was unglazed, he was afraid that they had no glass. But they had. They told him they had some beads of it, and knew it was used as decoration on 'some of the treasure'.

Cailan then asked if perhaps tomorrow Nial would show some of them his boat, and explain what the 'steel' thing on its floor was. It was a moment or two before Nial realised that he meant the outboard motor. Yes! That would cause quite a stir!

'My son,' said the Abbot, 'these things are of the future; your clothes, shoes, wonderful knife, and, I gather, your boat is unusual too. Would you not tell us how people will live in—when did you say it was?'

Nial looked round the crowded room, trying to size up what would be most interesting to his audience. But he could only guess. 'If I was to tell you everything about the twentieth century, I'm afraid you wouldn't like what you heard. But I'll try to do as you ask. To start with, I suppose people live in much bigger houses, that is, often bigger than your church, though perhaps not so colourful and certainly not so marvellously decorated. Often the buildings are tall—taller than your Bell House—and have many floors, maybe fifty or more; and there are great cities of them covering areas bigger than even the lough here.' His listeners were silent, every face of them turned intently towards him, every mouth sagging a little at his astounding words.

'People wear much more clothing than you do,' he continued, remembering the scantily but apparently quite normally clad boy in the Cooking House, not to mention his own present apparel. 'But if this afternoon was anything to go by, I think the weather you have is a good deal warmer than I am used to, though I can't imagine how, or why. We eat a lot of foreign food; stuff grown in "Australia" and "America".'

'Where, my son?' The Abbot looked puzzled.

Nial remembered the places would be unknown. 'Well, from all round the world, hot places . . .'

'*Round* the world? What do you mean?'

'From the other side . . . Oh, glory!' He realised with a jolt that they would think the world was flat, and he desperately started to explain. 'Well, you see, *we* have proved that the world is round—like an apple—you see, and there are foreign countries on the other side where it's very hot, and they have summer when we're having winter; and by keeping things cold and transporting them in very fast ships, we can have their fruit in winter—and our own in summer . . . I'm afraid that isn't awfully clear, but I'm doing my best!'

'I confess,' said the Abbot slowly, 'I can hardly follow the things you say. Could you please try again about the world being round? Why, supposing this to be so, do people not fall off the bottom of it?'

'Well,' said Nial, stifling a grin, 'because of "gravity".' His mind whirled. 'You know; when you lift a stone or something, it's heavy, and when you let it go, it falls. Well, though I've never been there myself, it's just the same on the other side of the world—things still fall towards the ground. I've seen "film" of it, and—oh dear!' Explaining film was even more difficult. By now everyone was sitting in a kind of stupor, and Nial began to feel sure they had taken about as much as they could. Then someone got up and asked the very question he had been dreading.

'With all these cities and things everywhere, what about here? Are there going to be many people living here?'

Nial felt his heart sinking in a series of ever-louder bumps, and in desperation he turned to Cailan. But Cailan was looking at him with the same pure interest of the questioner. Nial was on his own now. How *could* he tell them, when they had fed and clothed him, and made him welcome? And then his eyes met the Abbot's, and somehow he knew that he must tell the truth.

'No,' he said gently, 'not many people, not here exactly.'

There was a silence while everyone thought this out.

'The Danes,' said someone.

'Yes. A-at least, I think so.' Nial's relief at having the bad bit done for him gave him courage to say more. 'But they don't overcome your religion; in fact,' clutching at straws, 'I know you have already converted some of them.' The Danish twins nudged each other and looked pleased.

'We not the firsht,' said one of them. 'Abbot before our Abbot Sedna was Norse, too.'

The Abbot nodded. 'This is so, Nial. My predecessor was indeed a Norseman. He lived in the colony of Danes at the south of Lough Cuan, and went reeving with them too, plundering, burning, and fighting. As a lad of about your own age he was severely burned about the back and thighs when a playmate pushed him onto a smouldering fire. Somehow he got up off the fierce heat of the ashes and survived, though he lost for ever the full use of his left leg. Thereafter he was known as "Tholrykr", meaning "the endurer of smoke". Walking, and indeed still fighting with a tall stick under his arm for support, he was even then a fearsome figure, for he was broad like an ox, and tall, much taller than any of us; more than a double arm-span in height.' Nial had already noticed that his own five-foot-eight put him head-and-shoulders above most of these people, except for the dark Danish twins.

'This great powerful man was nevertheless much jeered at by his fellows, who had no time for even mildly disabled folk. This made him develop a violent temper and great skill with his weapons, so that he managed to get his own way. Thus, he was on one of the forays that went up the lough by longship, and over the land to attack and destroy many places of wealth and importance, and gain treasure in great quantity.'

Out of the corner of his eye, Nial could see that everyone was hunched keenly forward, some nodding as they followed what was obviously an often-repeated tale.

'With a considerable amount of loot on board the returning ship, they decided to stop off and bury some of it on one or two of the islands not far from here. Tholrykr and one other went ashore alone, ordering the rest to remain in the ship; and as there was much strong liquor amongst the remaining plunder, everyone was apparently happy enough with this arrangement. Afterwards even Tholrykr got drunk, for the digging proved to be thirsty work. And so it was that in the angry darkness of the open lough a quarrel broke out between himself and the other leaders, and the word is that he killed and wounded not a few of them before one even greater than he caught him off balance, and tipped him into the sea. At that moment they were steering inside the big island just to the south of us, called Treshnagh, (for in their drunkenness they had missed their way), and he swam across, not to it, but to the small island opposite that is connected to the mainland at low tide.' The old eyes sparkled, and the low voice softened a bit.

'When the day came, and he saw where he was, though

he could have walked home, Tholrykr stayed and thought of all the beautiful things that he had buried. And the more he thought, the more it occurred to him that people who would go to the lengths of living poorly and simply in order to spend time praying, and making with such infinite care and precision all those priceless and lovely things just to glorify their God, must indeed have a truly remarkable Deity to be worth such effort. Deciding then and there that he wanted to know more—and he had had enough of warfare and reeving anyway—he took his battle-axe which had been slung in his belt when he fell from the ship, and which, because he was a powerful swimmer despite his leg, had not weighed him down, and he buried it as a symbol of his decision. Indeed, we now call the place "Broad-Axe Island".' He used the Norse words fluently, so that they sounded remarkably like English to Nial.

'Of course, Tholrykr knew of our establishment here, even though in those days we had no tall Bell House and were not so conspicuous. He also knew that our symbol was a cross. So, fashioning one from two bits of driftwood, he crossed to the mainland when the tide was low, and hobbled along the shore holding it before him with his strongly developed right arm, working his stick with the weaker left. He was well aware of the colossal risk he was taking, for the local people will tear a Norseman to pieces should they find him alone and unarmed. But though he passed within two paces of a group of farmers, they did no more than look curiously at him, and he saw that the cross was making peace between them and him. When he came to the shore opposite us here, he waded out as best he could into the water, and stood with the tide rising about him, holding up his cross so that the monks should see him and know he came in peace. And so it was that a boat was sent for him, and he became one of us, with a great desire to know our God. And Tholrykr became a wise teacher who could read and write, not only our letters and language, but Latin and his own tongue too, and indeed he translated many books into the Norse.'

Abbot Sedna paused here, leaning back in the great, creaking chair, and flexing his elderly shoulders. Then he bent right forward as though confidentially, and looked Nial full in the face.

'Now, it so happened that he remembered the grand hoard of treasure; gems, much silver, and indeed even a small amount of river-gold, that his one-time fellow warrior and he had buried on the island they called "Lang-ey", the "Long Isle", which is not far from here over by the other side of the lough. One night he went there and dug some of it up. This he kept here for many years, until shortly after he had become Prime Abbot. And one day a man arrived who was none other than Colm, Son of Conaing, and the greatest metal worker of our time, as Aed will tell you. He has made many jewelled crosses in precious metals, and several shrines for books and for articles of clothing, belts and the like, of many saints, not to mention huge brooches for the kings themselves. But at that time he was still a young man, not older than Cailan here. Even so, Abbot Tholrykr saw the skill in him, and gave him the rich metals he had kept. Colm took these to his home, far to the south, and made for the glory of the Son of God and His twelve followers a great silver Communion cup, decorating in gold its stem, base and bands about its main body with the very finest of modern designs, such as have never been seen before or since, in these parts.

'This took Colm very nearly a year to complete, and just after he returned to Aendrum with the cup, a boy came from one of the islands, and watched Colm making a small brooch of bronze, and he expressed so much pleasure in it that Colm told him that if he would spend his life in the service of God, he could keep the brooch. And so Aed is still with us, and as you know makes fine things of that sort himself.

'But as for Abbot Tholrykr,' he continued, 'he gave the cup to Aendrum for use on special occasions, and we also have it still. Other riches from the buried hoard he gave to churches near and far, like that of Commar not far to the north-west, when their own had been lost or stolen. Some he was able to return to its original owners—those who had lived. And then one day there came a foreigner to the island, and he had a plague upon him, and not only he, but the Prime Abbot and most of our Brothers, died of it.'

For a moment the old man sat still, staring into the glowing embers of the dying fire. His voice was quiet with sadness when he spoke again.

'We buried them in the confines of the new stone church, every one of them; and they—they fitted—exactly. I have never been able to understand the miracle of that. There was not one unused space left under the floor, and yet each one was just clear of the other.' Sitting back, the old man rubbed the top of his bald head, and everyone sighed and shuffled at what was clearly the end of the story. But the Abbot spoke again, smiling now.

'So, Nial, my son, when you say that Aendrum is to die at the hands of the Danes, though the thought makes us sad, we are not too distressed. You also say our Faith shall live on. This is indeed what we have worked for, *and* what happened in the case of Abbot Tholrykr, for the works he translated into his own tongue fell into the hands of our enemies also, and yet bore fruit, in their own town by the Narrows of this lough. Our own twin Brothers found some fragments of one of the books, and having just learned to read, spelt out the words to each other. They came here, just the two of them, by boat one dark night, creeping over the island under the trees and by the water's edge lest the farmers found them. Our guard caught them trying to scale the outer cashel, and brought them before me. They showed me the torn remains they had brought with them, and I knew at once the hand of Tholrykr.

'No, my son. We are not dismayed at your news. No doubt such a thing will not happen for a time yet. But tell us, will there still be wars between men in the years to come?'

Nial was shaken back into the future, as it were, rather sharply.

'Oh yes, Abbot! I'm afraid there will be. Such wars as you have never dreamed possible. What weapons do you have?'

'Do not ask me of weapons, my son. Ask Aengus. He was once a seaman, and has travelled much, and seen many tools of war in his time. Speak up, Brother.'

Aengus looked over at Nial from the brown huddle of monks across the room, and the sharp eyes glittered in his wrinkled old face.

'Here we use only slings and staves, of course. But outside the monastery the islanders use the bow, short-sword and axe, and like our helpers are excellent hands with spears and knives. But across the water I have seen great war machines that I am told once hurled whole rocks.'

Nial stared at the dark clay floor.

'In the future there are to be far worse things than those,' he said softly. 'There will be "guns" and, more dreadful still, "bombs". Both of these make a noise like—well, like thunder. Come to think of it, they work rather like thunderbolts in a way. But some of them can, believe me or not, destroy in one brief moment those vast cities of great buildings I have told you about, they are so powerful.'

'Like Sodom and Gomorrah,' muttered someone.

'Something like that,' said Nial.

'Yet life goes on?' Cailan had an anxious look in his blue eyes.

'Though hundreds are killed at a time, yes, life goes on, somehow.'

'Ach, it is all so senseless! What good did ever a war do? What difference does it all make?'

'People are still asking that in my day, Cailan. But still they fight. I suppose you could say that many of the things invented first as weapons eventually are put to work in peaceful uses. Even the wild power of those great "bombs" can be tamed, and made to—oh, cure diseases and all sorts of things.'

'Swords into ploughs,' said the Abbot, more to himself than anyone else.

4

Outboards and Rudders

The sun, streaming at a low, golden slant through the doorway of Cailan's hut, and the last clang of the bell for Morning Prayers, together woke Nial. His watch told him it was barely four-thirty, but he felt remarkably fresh. Lying there watching a small, dark-coloured spider crawling busily among the straw thatch close above his head, he considered the fact that yesterday had obviously *not* been a dream. Outside, the singing of birds in the fruit trees that straggled over the eastern slope of the hill, and the horn-like moos of a cow by the outer cashel, competed with the deep voices of the monks which lilted joyfully from the paneless windows of the church. Cailan would be there.

He stretched, and a round little brown mouse scampered away and out of the door. Nial's teeth felt furry. He threw back the rugs, and reached for the pile of clothes. One thing in their favour; it didn't take long to dress. His gym-shoes took more time to put on than the rest of the outfit.

Only the guards were about as he strolled round the path between the inner and middle cashels and past the Eating House where the discussions of last night still rang, remark and phrase, in his mind. Ahead, and unlike any of the other buildings except the kitchen next to it, the rectangular School House projected inwards from the middle cashel. To a height of four or five feet, its walls were of rough stone. Above that the gable ends were coarsely plastered, and where this coating had broken away, their inner construction of mud blocks showed brownly through. The thick, nail-studded oak door stood open, invitingly.

What a school it was! Placed so as to receive the maximum amount of light from the narrow little windows, were a number of tables and benches. On them were short wooden boards like that which Nial had seen Abbot Sedna using in the Bell House, and looking more closely at one of them he now saw that a complete side was covered in a layer of wax on which someone had been practising the alphabet, scratching the squiggly letters on with the sharply-pointed iron stylus that lay next to it on the table.

'The bees make it.'

Nial spun round. In the corner behind the door stood the cook's young assistant, still wearing only the cloak, and that thrown back over his shoulders. He was holding what looked like a small piece of slate.

'Sorry,' gasped Nial, 'I didn't know anyone was here.'

'That's all right. Do you mind me talking to you?'

'Goodness, no. Why should I?'

'Because of you being from another time, and everything.' The boy looked down at the slate. 'Are you very holy?'

'Er—no, not especially.' Nial giggled. 'I feel perfectly normal, actually—and rather hungry.'

'Breakfast happens soon now, a bit after they come out. Haven't you seen waxboards before?'

'Waxboards? Oh. No, but they're a jolly good idea. I suppose you can clean them again quite easily? We use paper, made from pulped wood, for writing on.'

'You must be very rich, then! I wish I could draw like Trichem. Look—' and coming over to Nial, he held out the bit of slate. Scratched on its smooth surface were several of the knotwork patterns that seemed so popular, but what really caught Nial's eye was a set of small and quite perfect intersecting circles.

'Who's Trichem? And—hey! How did he do these?'

'Which? Oh, with these things.' The boy picked up a pair of very ordinary-looking, if slightly rusty dividers. 'He's my uncle's son. Of course, he's a lot older than me, but he *is* clever. I'm Dichu. My friends call me Mo-Dichu because they like me. Can I call you Nial?'

'Yes, of course. You help with the cooking, don't you?'

'By the Saints! The porridge!' and Dichu dropped the dividers on the table and fled through the door with his cloak flapping back from his skinny young shoulders.

Nial looked about himself again.

The other tables were also spread with slates and waxboards, all showing the results of trial and practice. There were wobbly sketches of various rather stylised birds and animals—one of the latter apparently a donkey pulling some kind of agricultural implement. One slate portrayed rows of a gradually improving letter 'e', while another showed several attempts at three-cornered knotwork patterns. There was a perfectly recognisable outline drawing of the school building itself, though the pupil had gone a bit wrong with the gable end. Another picture amused Nial a lot because the artist had been drawing a horse, and in starting at the head end, had run out of slate and simply bent the body and hind legs at right-angles, in order to complete it; some blinding logic persuading him that half a horse would only look ridiculous.

A row of little pots and a pile of seagull's wing-feathers on a smaller table at one end of the room proved to be simply a collection of coloured inks and pens, but the sheets of thick vellum on which they had been used made Nial stare in disbelief.

The combined effect of yellows, reds, blues, greens and bright purples filling the spaces between elaborate lettering in black, was quite dazzling even in the comparatively dim light coming through the narrow windows and reflecting from the embroidered linen hangings on the rough stone walls.

Nial heard voices outside, and went round to the Cooking House to see if Dichu needed a hand with carrying the food.

It was later in the morning, when on the rising tide he demonstrated *Cuan*'s outboard motor.

With Cailan leading the way down the east side of the hill, Nial and a number of the monks squeezed in single file through the slanting, narrow main entrance of the middle cashel, and past the well, below in the hollow. The final way through the tremendous width of the vast outer cashel was doubly complicated, but again obviously constructed with the same idea of making it impossible for more than one person to pass at a time. It came out at the head of a narrow ramp of earth and stones at one end of the great ditch separating the monastery from the rest of Mahee Island. Ahead lay the stone causeway along which the islanders could make their clearly visible approach, but Cailan turned sharp left and trotted down a steep little slope to the shore, heading round towards the point nearest to Island Reagh.

There were gasps when *Cuan* came into view, and everyone stared in wonder at the gleaming hull. They were quite delighted when, after he had fixed the outboard securely to the transom, Nial asked them to help launch her over the seaweed.

He motioned Cailan to join him, climbed aboard, and was preparing to start the motor when he saw Dichu standing wistfully in the background.

'Can he come too, Cailan?'

'Who? Ach, the lad! Aye, why ever not?'

So with the two of them sitting proudly on the varnished centre-thwart where they were safely out of his way, Nial pushed with an oar, and *Cuan* slid into deeper water. He lowered the motor into position, set the controls, and hoping everything had dried out after the swamping of yesterday, he pulled the starting cord. To his intense relief, there was a spluttering cough, and the engine burst into full, vibrant life. The monks, who had not been quite sure about what was going to happen anyway, and certainly hadn't expected a noise, were taken by complete and shattering surprise by the sudden explosion of roaring, rattling sound. As if the miraculous fact that the shining piece of metal was actually propelling the boat at considerable speed across the water was not more than enough for them, the continuous racket it emitted was terrifying to their ears. They had never heard anything even remotely like it. Some, wide-eyed and stumbling, took to their heels and ran; others went down on their knees; and before very long, more of them came leaping and racing over the stony beach and down the drumlin slopes from the monastery, to see what fantastic thing had arrived in their midst. Nial could even see people hanging out of the windows of the distant Bell House tower, and sea-birds from near and far rose shrieking in the air and flew off in all directions.

Cailan and young Dichu, who had been delighted at being allowed on board, now sat clutching each other up in the bows, pale and rigid with fright. Chortling to himself, but nevertheless taking pity on his petrified passengers, Nial at last slowed the motor down, and began turning the boat round in a gentle circle close in to the shore. Eventually Cailan began to smile uneasily, and then, as he gained confidence, he asked for more speed, and yet more, until again they were flying round, bounding over and through their own wake with spray all over the place and sending great waves curling up the beach among the feet of the incredulous crowd. Dichu crouched low on the floorboards, wanting to hold on and yet not daring to take his hands away from over his ears.

Fortunately, in view of what was to happen later, it at last dawned on Nial that until he and his boat returned to the twentieth century, he would be unable to obtain further supplies of petrol, so he hurriedly headed in and stopped the motor, running *Cuan*'s nose gently up on to the soft seaweed. Dichu and Cailan leapt out.

The brief silence that followed somehow seemed violent; and then everyone crowded forward to get a closer look at what they were already calling 'the Fire Iron', for like most two-stroke engines it had released a thin trail of blue smoke. They were all talking at once, asking how it worked, what kept it going so long without drawing breath, why it made such a racket, how the fire had lit itself, and so on, until there was a sudden yelp and somebody reeled back vigorously shaking the hand he had just burnt by touching an exposed part of the exhaust system. Nial hastened over to offer his apologies, and found himself staring into the startled grey eyes of the Prime Abbot himself.

'I'm most terribly sorry,' he exclaimed. 'I quite forgot you wouldn't know it was hot!'

'Nonsense, my son! It makes smoke enough for all to see! It is I who should apologise for being stupid! Serves me right for being so inquisitive.'

Then the questions started again, and as best as he could, Nial explained the basic principles of the internal combustion engine. When he finished off with a hand-turned demonstration of how the blades of the propeller revolved, and so thrust the boat along, he got the impression that that was the only bit that anyone had understood.

'It certainly is a marvellous invention,' said the Abbot thoughtfully. 'I wonder if Critan could copy it. Or is it also made from that "steel" stuff you told us of?'

'I think it is, Abbot. But anyway there would be no "petrol" to run it on.'

'"Petrol", my son?'

'Yes, the liquid that—er, that it burns. It's a sort of oil that comes from foreign countries.'

'Oh, but we have some of that! It is expensive, of course, but for use in frightening away the Danes, as I am sure it would . . .'

'But Abbot, I thought—well, that "petrol" wasn't, that is *won't* be discovered for ages yet?'

'Oh, but I assure you, my son. We do not call it that, but the oil I am speaking of must be the same thing. Indeed, it comes from very far away. Smells a bit of hazel-nuts, though I believe it is made from "olives", whatever that might be. It grows on a hill near the Holy City, you know.'

Nial with a great effort managed to retain a fairly serious expression, and reached down to unscrew the filler cap on the motor's small black tank.

'Does it smell like this?'

But the Prime Abbot of Aendrum, having been as it were bitten once already by the strange device, was more cautious now.

'I—er, have a slight cold, my son. Perhaps Cailan would be good enough to—er, thank you, Brother!'

Cailan sniffed deeply over the hole and recoiled in horror.

'Faugh! Heugh! Ach! PHOO!'
Everyone laughed.
'Not hazel-nuts, Brother?'
'Not! No! Nor anything else we know! Ach! Sickly-sweet and quite dreadful! Now I know why it shakes and roars so, if it feeds on that stuff!'

'Ah, well.' The Abbot tapped the finger-tips of both hands together, and sighed. 'Perhaps it is no harm. There do seem to be certain risks attached to the handling of such things! But what other objects do you have to show us from the age to come, Nial? Or do I mean *for*? Dear me!'

Nial replaced the petrol cap and did it up tightly to avoid evaporation, and began to remove the engine from the stern.

'I am not entirely sure what else I have,' he said slowly. 'You see, before I—"came" here, if you see what I mean, I did spend a night aboard my father's boat over beyond the other side of that island. Since my boat and the "motor" came with me, I suppose that too just *might* still be there somewhere.'

'If it is,' said the Abbot, 'you would naturally want to bring it here for safety. But I thought you lived in houses? Boats are terribly draughty and damp.'

'Oh no,' said Nial. 'You see, she's made of "fibreglass" and doesn't leak. Oh—that's a sort of "plastic", or rather, *was*.'

'Will be,' said Cailan.

'Or,' the Abbot nodded, 'indeed could, as our friend says, still be. You must find out, my son! Yes, you must find out right away about your father's boat. I imagine it is longer than this wonderful one of your own. It will be quite marvellous, I am sure. Go now, before the Danes find it. You shall take Cailan with you though. It is not safe to go alone, and if you see a Danish ship you must return at once. That Fire

Iron thing should keep you ahead of them without difficulty! Dichu may perform you a service by fetching some food for the two of you to eat as you go.'

'It's all right,' said Nial, suddenly remembering the dufflebag with its uneaten food. 'I have plenty in the boat. But has Cailan enough time? I mean, has he no duties or anything?'

'My son, Cailan is excused all but the most important duty—which is to look after you and your needs until the time comes when you can show us your Purpose here.'

The thin sound of the bell jangling distantly over the island meant that Nial and Cailan were soon left on their own to rig *Cuan*, while the crowd dispersed rapidly up over the slope and back to the shingle-roofed church.

'You need not fear,' said Cailan conversationally, 'they will be praying for us, so we will return safely. What is this black iron thing?'

'Oh, that's the centre-plate. For sailing—goodness! Don't you have them?'

'Well, no. You see mostly we row in the lough here, though we do have one boat with a sail. Our skin-covered craft are lighter than this *Cuan* of yours, so such a heavy thing would not be good. What does it do, anyway?'

'Goes down that slotted case there, and—well, it stops the boat slipping sideways when you're sailing her into the wind. Being so heavy it also helps to hold her up a little too, I suppose.'

'Did you say "*into*" the wind?'

'Yes—why, of course! If you don't know about keels your boats must only be able to sail with the wind astern, or at best coming from abeam!'

'Just forward of it in favourable conditions; but surely

you do not mean *Cuan* can actually sail *into* the wind?' Cailan bent over to finger the edge of the plate, while Nial loosed the sail preparatory to hoisting it.

'Not *straight* into the wind, of course, because naturally you couldn't fill the sail, and it would just flap like a flag and not drive. But quite close all the same. By heading first this way and then that, you can eventually reach a point that is in fact right upwind of where you started.'

'Ach, never! However can the wind blow a boat back up against itself?'

Now, Nial had never thought of it that way, so he told Cailan to wait and see. With the breeze still in the east like this, they would probably have some windward work in order to sail out into the open lough.

Suddenly he turned to his friend again.

'We can't get out, anyhow!'

'Why ever not?'

'Because the tide's still flooding, and while she just might go fast enough to overcome the current in the narrows with the wind aft, she'd never do it "beating".'

'But it does not run all that strongly! Why, we often row through against it. And if you prefer, we can always go out by here, though it is surely a long way round!'

Nial saw that he was pointing to the gap separating them from Island Reagh, and at that moment realised just why the current in the main narrows to the south of them would indeed run with less force than he had experienced on his way in. With no man-made causeways blocking the many other entrances between the islands, the tide now had a free run, instead of having to squeeze its entire volume through just two swirling sounds.

They pushed away, and Nial shoved with an oar to clear

Cuan from the weed-packed shallows, and then rowed her out into deeper water.

'I could be doing that,' said Cailan from the stern. 'Though your oars look different to ours and sit in those iron things instead of being held by wooden pins, the action looks just the same.'

'It's all right, thank you. We'll make sail in a moment. Just want to get into deep enough water for the centre-plate.'

'Ach, it is just that I feel rather helpless. But what with your Fire Iron and this elaborate sail with all its strange fitments, looking so complicated and new to me, I feel lost for a way of being useful.'

'Well, if you've sailed at all, you will know to sit on the windward side, to help balance the boat against the pressure of the wind. Here—stow these oars under the "thwart" while I hoist the sail.'

'By "thwart", I take it you mean this seat? And I *do* know about keeping boats upright under sail. My uncle and I sailed most of the way here from Iona. And now that I think of it, did we not have a wind from the same airt as today's, the whole way to the Straights of Moyle.'

'Is your uncle at Aendrum? I didn't know.'

'Ach no. He is himself an Abbot of some importance, and presides at a monastery many days to the south of here, some say near the very centre of this land. Its founder had the same name as my uncle, strangely enough.'

'Have you been there?'

'No indeed. But I wish to see it one day. I believe it is not unlike Aendrum; fortified the same way, and also on an island.'

'An island?'

'Aye, in Lough Ree. Uncle Dairmid likes islands, just as I do myself.'

Nial gave the halyard a final tweak to swig the fluttering canvas the last inch up the mast, made fast, and then lowered the heavy centre-plate into its case. Cailan meanwhile eyed the black painted rudder and gleaming oak tiller that lay on the floorboards, but their purpose completely eluded him until Nial bent over the stern and shipped them in their place.

'Ach! A device for steering! Now *there* is an idea! You must show Ailil that.'

'Ailil?'

Cailan put his slim hand on the free-swinging tiller. 'Our carpenter. He builds all our boats, but steers them with an oar. My, but this is much better!'

Nial pulled in an inch or two of mainsheet, tightening in the sail, until it filled to the breeze and *Cuan* began to move. She gathered speed and caused the tiller to spring to life. Doubt spread across Cailan's face, but Nial grinned.

'Pull it towards you a bit. That's it. Now she'll go!' And indeed the little boat commenced to reach rapidly along in the sun-sparkled water, heading roughly parallel to the Mahee shore. The young monk at her helm was beaming with delight at the easy way she handled, responding to his lightest touch on the strange arrangement under his hand. Nial, seated on the centre-thwart in his white tunic, and almost subconsciously altering the trim of the sail to suit the rather wandering course being steered, was gazing up the sloping ground of the island to the high stone defences, the cluster of thatched, shingled and stone roofs, and above all, the tall, space-rocket shape of the Bell House. Things from a thousand years ago! And here he was sailing his twentieth-century boat in the midst of it all.

The sail shook violently, and *Cuan* lurched.

'Ach! Sorry!'

'No, no.' Nial hastily pulled in the slack sheet, and the sail quietened. 'Entirely my fault. I was thinking about—Well, let's say I wasn't thinking.'

'I am Celtic,' said Cailan.

'Meaning?'

'Meaning I know what you were thinking.' He nodded towards the monastery. 'You have seen it in ruins. Have you not?'

'Must we talk about it? Look, we're coming round to the narrows and we'll have to sail to windward. I'd better take her, if you don't mind.'

'Not at all. I still have not grasped the principle of that. Here you are. Do you want me to manage the sail for you?'

'No, thanks. But if you sit well up to windward it would help a lot. The breeze is quite fresh.'

'It often is just here. Something to do with the gap between the islands. Old Finnian had our best boat over in a gust just last week! It did him no good whatever. Why he was sailing, I have not discovered, but fortunately the tide was slack and he and the boat drifted ashore. Finnian is the brother of Aengus, whom you met in the Bell House. They were both deep-water men, before they joined us. Poor old Finnian was so ashamed of himself at going over, and I think Aengus has practically disowned him!' Cailan chuckled to himself at the thought. 'Saints! But your boat does go up close to the wind! Oh, if only ours would sail like this, we could outstrip the Danes every time!'

'Do you often come across them, then?' Nial hauled in his sheet, and *Cuan* sliced along in fine style.

'Too often, alas. Not so much us, because we do most of our fishing inside the islands, but the other folk of the lough. Ach, it has not been too bad recently, but every so often some of the younger ones lie in wait behind one or other of the higher islands, with a man up on the sky-line watching for you. Sometimes all you see of him will be his head above the long grass—then an arm is raised, and in a moment a horde of howling murderers come sailing round the point; an axe is thrown, and that is that. They call it "fishing".'

'Why fishing?' Nial was somewhat horrified.

'All they want is your catch. But they are lazy, and apparently consider it more fun that way.'

'You mean they'd murder you for a few little fish?'

'Ach now, the fish are very good, and big too. Yes, I do mean that. Are we not getting rather close to the shore for that iron plate thing?'

'Yes, close enough. We'll tack now.' And Nial swung *Cuan*'s head round so that her bow passed through the wind's eye in a single, sweeping movement. Cailan was fascinated. The sail fluttered briefly before filling again on the new tack, and the two of them slid their weight over to the starboard side.

Cuan headed out into deeper water, and began to fight her way over the flooding current. She gained what was to both of them a surprising amount, making right up into the bay on Mahee. The latter at first looked rather empty to Nial, who remembered it lined with bungalows and boathouses and a small slipway and wooden pier. Then he saw a low, weed-covered boulder jetty, and upside down on the beach and looking like stranded whales, a pair of extremely fine skin boats, each about twenty to twenty-five feet long. He jerked his head in their direction.

'Monastery boats?'

'Aye, our best. The left-hand one has made the trip to Iona. A grand seaboat.'

Nial once more tacked the dinghy and began to head her out towards the open lough.

Cuan slowed now as they reached through the channel in the lee of little Calf Island. The wind failed for a second or two, and Nial was pleased to see Cailan automatically shift towards the centre of the boat, keeping her just slightly heeled so that the sail lay quietly and didn't swing inboard. Ahead, the blue water of the lough stretched away to the south and east, its dark crinkled surface interrupted by the rounded, sunlit humps of the islands. Nial eased the sheet and began to steer round to the right. Cailan, sitting bolt upright with the freshened breeze now blowing the long fair hair across his face, slowly and carefully scanned the entire surroundings.

'It is all right. We can go,' he said.

'Eh?'

'The Danes.'

'What about them?'

'There are none about.'

'Oh. Oh, I see what you mean! Well, thank goodness for that! I'd quite forgotten them again.' Nial found it very hard to think of his native County Down being over-run by foreign marauders. To start with, he had never considered Denmark as an enemy country. Again and again he found himself fighting a mental battle, not with them, but with his own mind, desperately trying to get used to the still incredible idea that he really *was* existing in the tenth century, and that this man at his side must have been dead, and presumably buried, over nine hundred years before he, Nial, was born. But it was all real enough. It must be.

Whiterock Bay was empty. Not a boat, even of this ancient period, was in sight. The breeze-ruffled water lapped in its timeless way on the weed-burdened stones of the foreshore where the smooth slipways and crowded dinghy parks should or would project their straight, angular edges far out over it.

No whitened flag-poles, no tapping of halyards on countless masts, no bungalows, no cars. No people, either—unless... Yes! There was someone—running along the shore just below a tangle of briars near the Bradock Island side of the bay. A dim figure, whose pale buff garment blended almost to vanishing point against the background. It was only the movement that made him visible, racing along, leaping deftly over the uneven beach.

'What's bothering him, Cailan?'

'Who? Ach, I see him now—aye indeed, he does seem in a hurry.'

'Could it be *Cuan*?' Nial remembered how strange his boat had first seemed even to Cailan. 'Maybe he thinks we're the Danes.' But Cailan was again staring round, and suddenly stiffened and with a sharp intake of breath he clapped a hand on to Nial's arm.

'Look!' He did not point. His steady gaze was easy to follow. Out beyond Bradock and well clear of the larger island of Conly a little to the southeast, was a sight that was to imprint itself on Nial's mind for always. Bow-on, with her broad, red-and-white striped sail angled to the wind and the flared-out topsides of her high, curving prow tumbling a creamy bone before them, came a Viking ship. No, it was no use blinking. The thing was there. Nial gulped.

'Nial.' Cailan's voice was level, controlled. 'Get us behind Broad-Axe Island. Quickly.'

'S-she must have seen us!'

'Not necessarily. I remember Ranvaig telling me that you cannot easily see directly forward in those craft unless you are standing in the bows. We have a chance—if we can just beach *Cuan* and run for it.'

'No!' Nial banged the helm over and the boat lurched as

the boom came slamming across in an all-standing gybe.

'What are you doing!'

'In there!' Nial fought with tiller and sheet to get *Cuan* on course for the gap between Rainey and Sketrick Island. 'If we go that way we'll not only stay dead ahead of them as they point now, but we'll not be sideways on! They may not see us even if they are looking!'

'If they do, they will follow! It will lead them to Aendrum!'

Nial looked at him. 'We'll have to risk that.'

'But . . .'

'Cailan—I want to keep *Cuan*.'

Cailan's blue eyes stared at him, then at the longship. Then they softened into a remarkably sunny smile.

'You are right. Of course you are! Who is afraid of Danes, anyhow!—I have just noticed they are not rigged for war.'

'Rigged for war?'

'Aye. No shields along the ship's sides. I cannot guess what they are doing up this way, of course, but they are not *looking* for trouble. It would be unwise of them to land anywhere here, and they must know that.'

Nial glanced astern over his shoulder. 'Well, why are they stuck head to wind?'

'Their boats do not sail into the breeze like this one, my friend. If they are wanting to turn and say, cruise along the shores of our own island for instance, they would have to row. They will be lowering their sail.'

'Do they often go along there?'

'No indeed. But they are quite safe in doing so. When the Danes go afloat, all other boats leave the lough's ways clear for them. Sail on, and watch.'

It was true. Long oars were being thrust through holes in

the Viking's sides. Four only could be seen on the side nearest them. Nial put his helm up slightly as *Cuan* neared the sheltering land.

'They do seem short-handed. I thought those things had hundreds of oars.'

'Not hundreds; thirty or forty, sometimes. I think they will soon be on their way. You know, they must have got in behind that island while you were showing us the Fire Iron. It was indeed distracting! Normally a good watch is kept from the Bell House.'

Already *Cuan* was well tucked into the sound between the two islands, and the flood tide was bearing them ever more rapidly in and round the corner. Their last sight of the longship showed her rowing steadily eastwards, the oars catching the sunlight as they flashed regularly up and down.

As Nial ran his bow gently up the Mahee beach just above the boulder jetty, several brown-robed monks came hurrying down from the cashel gateway to help them. They were in a state of some excitement.

'We saw the Danes appear, and we feared for you,' said one of them, rather surprisingly taking Nial's hand as they walked up the slope to the monastery.

5

The Treasure of Aendrum

Supper that evening surprised Nial by being mainly composed of shell-fish of various sorts; blue-grey slithery-looking things. He thought he recognised something the shape of a common mussel—the rest for the most part seemed to be small oysters. He didn't like them much, but felt full enough when the meal was over, and just a bit light-headed too. The drink offered was certainly very good. Its sweet, scented flavour blended so well with the unusual food.

Towards the end of the meal, someone came in and spoke to Cailan. Nial felt his shoulder being tapped.

'The Prime Abbot wants you.'

Nial started.

'Me? Why?'

Cailan stood up. 'Come on, I will tell you as we go.'

Nial followed out into the dusk, and they set off round to the gateway of the inner cashel. Ahead the tall needle of the round tower pointed darkly up among the first stars, and a dim light shone yellowly from the lowest window.

At the base of the ladder Cailan paused, and in that strange way of his, tilted his head over one shoulder. 'Nial,' he whispered seriously, 'I do not know what is in the Prime Abbot's mind; few people ever do; but what he is going to do is rare—unheard of, in fact. No outsider has ever before seen our Treasures.'

'Treasures? You mean, that Norse Abbot's...'

'Just so. It seems he is going to show them to you.'

'Oh!' said Nial, not quite sure what to say.

The monk threw the folds of his cloak back over his shoulders and climbed up the creaking ladder into the golden light issuing from the narrow doorway, bowed to the white figure of Abbot Sedna on reaching the tiny interior, and stood aside for Nial.

'Ah, my son.' The Abbot's deep voice rumbled round the shadowy walls as Nial ducked his way through the door. 'I am glad you are still with us; for a while this afternoon I feared we were going to lose you, *and* the good Cailan, to the foreigners. You did not find the boat of your parents?'

'No, Abbot.'

'Mmm. However, maybe you saw where it, er, should be? Did the place not stir in your memory any message for us?'

'Message? No; not that I know of.'

The Abbot stood up, small and slender, and lifted the smoking clay lamp off the tripod-rest that stood on the little table. 'My son, I have been thinking. It might help us to find out what your Purpose here is, if you were shown everything that we have. Come,' he said, and commenced to climb, somehow managing to keep one hand free for holding the lamp, which as it disappeared through the overhead opening plunged the room into sudden darkness. Nial started after him up the vertical ladder, and was surprised when Cailan did not follow. On the next floor a pile of straw with one rough blanket spread neatly upon it curved round part of the stone wall, and the Abbot eased his thin and elderly frame gently down on to it, having carefully placed the lamp on a wooden stand in the middle of the room. His long sinewy hand patted the blanket, and his low voice quietly boomed in the small space. 'Sit you here, son of Ross.'

Nial sat down on the bed. Not unnaturally he had expected to sink into the straw, so he was rudely shaken by being brought up short against solid wood. There seemed to be barely an inch of straw over it. The Abbot cocked an eyebrow at him, and smiled slightly.

'I try to live straight, my son; and that means sleeping straight.' He scratched himself. 'There is, however, more in this bed than meets the eye.'

For a moment Nial wondered if he meant like the mice that apparently lived in Cailan's bedding, but as he watched, the Abbot bent down and lifted away a whole section at one side of the pile of straw, the latter being carefully attached to a piece of board. A dark brown, almost black bag that clonked metallically was dragged out, and its neck gently unfolded. The Abbot paused dramatically, then fished in the bag and withdrew what appeared to be a model of Noah's Ark, and handed it reverently to Nial. Closer inspection showed that it was intended to represent a building, not a boat. Its main surfaces were clearly made from thin sheets of bronze, with heavy silver ornamentation. About six or eight inches long and three wide, its "roof" slanted steeply up on each side, terminating in a ridge-pole of solid silver worked in semi-relief in a neat confusion of the same knotwork patterns that Nial had seen so much of elsewhere, on walls, slates, wood and stone. The lower edges of the roof were also done in a thick band of silver, this time criss-crossed adn dotted with minute stipples so that it cleverly represented the cut-off ends of thatch. One corner had become badly worn, and the bronze covering was broken, revealing an inner layer of fine-grained wood.

'It is very nice,' said Nial, rather puzzled as to its purpose.

'Take the roof off, my son, but carefully; its contents are quite irreplaceable.'

With great care, Nial put the thing on his lap and pulled gently at the sloping lid. It was heavier than he had imagined, but came off easily.

The space inside the wooden lining of the box was filled with small things, so that it had the general appearance of a work-basket. There was a splinter of pale, slightly reddish wood, a scrap of dirty-looking cloth with a dark blotch on it, a little roll of some kind of parchment yellowing with age, and a finger ring, gold, but with a rounded oval stone shining in a dim blueness to the bobbing yellow light of the lamp.

'What are they? The ring looks lovely.'

'It is more than lovely! It is the ring of Mohee himself, made for him by a local expert.'

'What is the bit of wood?'

The Abbot's back lengthened by several inches and his voice rose, urgent with fervent excitment: 'Ah! Do not touch that, I beg of you!' He sank back as Nial drew his hand away in surprise at the sudden outburst. 'The Saints pity my forgetfulness in not warning you! I do not often show people these things. Why, that is a morsel of the dreadful Cross on which Jesus Himself was murdered! Almost a thousand years old, that is, and very dry and brittle. Every Abbey has a bit, you know. It would never do if we were to lose it! Indeed, I have often felt that if anything should happen to it, Aendrum itself would die for ever.'

Nial stared at the dusty chip and realised with a considerable jolt that Abbot Sedna had probably come as near to making a prophecy as he ever would. Aendrum was to die; he *wished* he knew when. Not that there were very great chances of this fragment really being a piece of the Cross, especially if the Abbot was right and every monastery had a bit of its own.

Just the same, the tiny object was obviously held in the deepest reverence.

'And the bit of cloth?'

'As old, my son, just as old. That is none other than part of the very garment He was wearing,' intoned the Abbot proudly. 'There are not many bits of that about, I can tell you! Do you not see the Precious Blood dried on it? Truly, that is one of our most prized relics.' And again there was not a scrap of doubt in the low-spoken words. It seemed to Nial that even in the tenth century there were 'wide boys' somewhere, trading 'genuine antiques' which they had probably made themselves.

The Abbot now reached into the box himself and gingerly took out the narrow roll of parchment. Because of its age, he explained, it was no longer safe to unroll it to the extent of flattening it out, but it was nevertheless possible to look at it in the form of a scroll, bit by bit, as it were. Inked on to its faintly mud-coloured surface was one of the most complicated designs Nial had ever seen, in a pastel violence of blues, mauves, browns, blacks, reds, and brilliant buttercup shades that seemed to glow, even in the small amount of light available. The entire work was so minute that the weaving, intersecting lines of colour were only just visible, and yet by skilful use of plain blocks of open space, the artist had managed to make the whole pattern come alive and dance joyously over the page. As it unrolled in the long hands of the Abbot, Nial watched four main panels emerge, each containing a separate and highly stylised, though recognisable, picture. There was a fair-haired, clean-shaven man dressed in blue and purple robes with curly hems. He was holding a slender, rather flowery-looking cross. Then there was a strange and very skinny beast that with a bit of imagination just might have been a lion, a thing that looked like a cow the wrong way up and tinted bright blue, and finally an extremely sad-looking bird, whose neck and head appeared to be quite bald. Each one of these figures was possessed of a vivid red and yellow halo and a pair of long, stiff, and drooping wings—the cow-creature had two pairs.

Underneath all this decoration there was row upon row of tiny writing, so neatly formed that at first Nial thought it was more lines of knotwork.

Seeing his amazement, the old man beamed with pleasure. 'Beautiful work, is it not? On this single scroll are written the four gospels. Every word is there, inked on, so I am told, with the hair of a mouse. Alas, I can no longer read it, though I could once.'

'What are the four pictures, Abbot?'

'My!' The glittering eyes opened wide in surprise, and stared at Nial owlishly. 'I thought the son of Ross said he was a Christian? Do you not know the emblems of Matthew, Mark, Luke and John, when you see them? Do you not go to school in the twentieth century?'

'Well, yes, we do. But I don't think such symbols are used any more, though it's a pity. They're rather fun.'

'But without pictures, how do the ordinary folk understand things?' The Abbot scratched the shiny top of his head. For a moment Nial didn't get the point, and then suddenly it dawned on him.

'Oh, of course! Well, in my day everyone can read, because schooling is compulsory.'

'Everyone? You mean, even the slaves?'

The word jarred. Somewhat shaken, Nial explained that no one in his Ireland had slaves, but that yes, everyone went to school, no matter how rich or poor they were.

'And who pays for the poor?'

'The state does.'

The Abbot looked at him blankly.

'From taxes and things.'

'The Danes! They are still with you, then!' The wrinkled face was crestfallen.

'No, they aren't! What made you think that?'

'The taxes. You mention taxes. No one takes taxes here but the Danes. The monastery pays heavily, simply to protect itself. But I sometimes wonder if it really does give us security.'

'In my day, that sort of thing is known as a "protection racket", and heavily frowned on by the authorities. No, the "State" I speak of is run by a group of people supposed to be picked by the population as a whole, and it supplies all sorts of benefits, like free medicine, help for old folk, schools for the young, and so on. It builds all the roads and things too. Most of them anyway.'

'It must be wealthy indeed. But I feel certain they have no treasure as wonderful as this;' and reaching down into the dark bag, he produced the oddest looking bowl that Nial had ever set eyes on. 'Prime Abbot Tholrykr's chalice,' announced the old man in a deep and reverent rumble.

Now Nial had always thought of chalices as being tallish, goblet-shaped vessels, made of silver. This one, he saw at once, was also made of silver, but there the resemblance ended abruptly. Standing on a widely splayed conical base which rose from a sort of flat flange, was a squat but quite lovely bowl. About nine or ten inches in diameter, it had a heavy lip and two broad and tightly radiused semicircular handles. It took Nial's breath away. The thing was liberally encrusted with gold, glass, and what appeared to be enamel, built up in a series of bands, medallions and bosses, in a manner that spoke most eloquently of skill, artistry and love.

The Abbot put it, very carefully, into Nial's slightly trembling hands. It was surprisingly heavy. He turned it on its side to study more closely the truly beautiful decoration.

As he was coming to expect, the bands of design were divided with great precision into a number of panels, and each panel had, standing out on its surface of gold foil, a different pattern made of intertwined gold wires, twisted and fixed into place with such fine and delicate care that in the lamplight they looked almost as if they had been cast there or even carved from the solid. At its neck, where the base joined the bowl, was yet another wide band, overlapping both parts, and again profusely worked in a fantastic series of criss-cross, under-and-over knotwork designs, and panels of spirals and exciting patterns of glittering yellow gold.

The handles were deeply inlaid with glass and enamel among delicate lines of silver, and the medallions, four of them, dotted round the belly, were similarly studded so that they glowed and sparkled like dull fires. Then, as the lamp flame reflected on the smooth silver body, Nial suddenly noticed a number of tall, rather spiky letters, clear among a border of fine dots round the outer part of the bowl, about half way down.

'What does it say?' he asked, his voice hushed.

'The names of the Apostles, my son. Is it not marvellous?' The Abbot's low tones sounded to Nial somehow in keeping with the wonderful thing he held.

'I have never seen anything like it—not even remotely like it,' he said. 'In fact, I doubt if anything quite so remarkable will ever be made again.'

The inside of the Chalice, by shattering contrast to its

elaborate exterior, was completely plain. Nial asked why it had not been worked too, so that one would see the decoration while in the act of drinking. The old Abbot showed genuine astonishment.

'But, my son, that would never do! If the inside was inscribed even lightly, it would be almost impossible to clean out, and the wine must be pure, you know. Have you not noticed how even our cooking pots are smooth on the inside, whatever designs our potter has thought fit to cut and mould on the outside? But the glory of *this* is not entirely hidden as one drinks! Whereas for him who receives the sacrament at the altar there is the moment of complete satisfaction as the blessed wine flows in his throat, taking with it the Holy Spirit and bursting into Sacred Fire in his belly, it is God who sees the beauty of the upturned cup, and is pleased by it. Look, give me the vessel.'

Nial gingerly handed it over, and with spritely agility Abbot Sedna O'Deman got down on his knees by the bed, and facing Nial, raised the great cup to his lips as though to drain it. Nial gasped out loud. On the underside of the deep conical base were again several panels of very fine interwoven silver mesh, and right in the centre, under the cup itself, was a protruding mound of clear polished crystal that glowed and shone as though lit from within. He stared at it in speechless silence. What can you say, he thought, in praise of a thing like that?

Slowly the old man lowered the heavy vessel, rested back on his heels, and reached for the dark cloth bag. As he put the chalice tenderly away, together with the strange box, he looked at Nial in a kindly, yet unsmiling way. Something clinked in the bottom of the bag, and his expression promptly changed.

'Och, me!' he said loudly. 'I nearly forgot to show you this! It was the very brooch worn by Abbot Tholrykr himself. Look; a grand piece of work, is it not?' And getting up, he held out a silver ring-brooch, the ends of which, and the sliding part of the long pin, were worked into round prickly balls which looked like part of a thistle-flower. In a way it was similar to the little one that Cailan wore, except that the split circle of this one was about three inches in diameter.

'It's enormous!' said Nial.

'You think so, my boy?' The Abbot smiled, making the thin skin of his face crinkle into a hundred merry lines. 'Then you want to see the brooches they make nowadays for the great kings and mighty warriors. Why, some of the pins of those ones are as long as my forearm, hand and all! And the great curves of the rings are so worked and inlaid as to put even our chalice somewhat in the shadows!'

'You couldn't be serious about that,' said Nial emphatically, 'nothing could be more tastefully decorated than the chalice.'

'Ah, quite right, my son. Quite right! Indeed I said nothing about the quality of the design. To my mind those great brooches look as brash and heathen as their wearers. To have seen our chalice is to know a standard by which all other art may be judged.' He stopped, and looked thoughtfully into Nial's face.

So long and steady was the gaze the Nial began to get embarrassed.

Then the Abbot spoke again. 'If ever,' he said gently, 'if ever it should be in your power, my son, to make it possible for the cup to be preserved for other men—perhaps in other times—to see, to wonder at, to think on, just as you and I have done tonight, do your very best.'

'I—I will, Abbot. But I truly hope that'll never happen! I should be terrified of the responsibility!'

'With God beside you at every step? Fear would melt into excitement, and would never trouble you! Besides, if those who fight against our cause knew you had it, you would hardly have time to be afraid!'

And the Abbot busied himself in putting the brooch back with its priceless fellows in the bag, the bag back under the bed, and the side of the bed back into place, so that not even Nial could see how it had come apart.

The Treasures of Aendrum were hidden once more.

6

Lady of the Herb Garden

As Cailan led Nial round, showing him the huts and cells of the monks, they passed Ranvaig and Shetelig busy cutting the long grass that grew from the earthen rampart of the middle cashel. Their brawny arms swung the odd little sickles with a rhythm of alternate swishes that was most pleasing to listen to. Nearby, Aengus and his brother were busily whirling the upper stones of a pair of hand-querns set up on a raised slab. A screen of drying cow-hides slung over poles served to keep the gentle wind from blowing away the coarse wholemeal flour that spilled like a creamy liquid from between the rumbling stones. From far down among the trees below them came the most delightful tinkling of bells, and Nial was thinking that there must be quite a large herd of goats, when all of a sudden, out from the shade of a fruit tree stepped, not a goat, but a majestically antlered deer, from whose red-brown neck hung a small bronze bell that *tink-tonked* with every pace of his slender front legs.

'Goodness, Cailan! Do you have many of those?'

'Which? Ach, the deer! Aye, well—not so very many really, for we have not as much grazing as we would like; but about thirty, I should think. Why?'

'Thirty? In my day you would be hard pressed to find that number in the whole of County Down!'

'I—er, do not know where that is.'

'No, of course you don't,' muttered Nial apologetically.

'Well, you're in it. It is what we call all this part of the country down to and including the Mournes.'

Cailan's head tilted questioningly again.

'The Mourne Mountains—those big ones you can see from here on a clear day. Don't say they've gone too!'

'Ach yes, I know now,' nodded Cailan, and he laughed. 'But whatever happened to the deer? Everyone of any standing has a herd of deer!'

Nial looked at him. 'What do you use them for?'

'To eat, of course, when food is scarce in the winter. It is good to get such rich and tasty meat.'

'Exactly,' said Nial. 'Too many people must have had the same idea at some time, and they were killed off faster than they could breed.'

'Bad management,' announced Cailan firmly. 'They are the most useful creatures! And you mean to tell me your father does not have a herd of them? But their hides are excellent for all sorts of things, shoes particularly; and as for the horns, well, they are ideal when planting things, working the soil over, ach, and building walls and all sorts of jobs. I suppose you will tell me now that in your time there will be machines like your Fire Iron to do all that?'

'Er, yes, there are. Will be.' Nial grinned sheepishly. 'And a lot of other things besides.'

'Is there anything you have not got machines for?' The almond-shaped eyes glinted mischievously. 'I know! You have not got machines that shave your beards!' Then, when Nial burst out laughing, the look of doubt returned to the monk's young face. 'Or perhaps no men shave any more?'

'O—Oh yes, they do,' spluttered Nial, 'at least most of them do! I'm laughing because we do have machines for even that!' His hand strayed to his own youthfully smooth chin. 'Not that I need one much yet. But we do have them.'

'My! But surely life must get awfully boring? Whatever do you do with yourselves, while all these machines are working for you?'

'Worry,' said Nial flatly.

'Worry?'

'Yes, worry. About how we shall manage if one or more of our wonderful machines break down and won't work any more! I wish all the people from my time could come here and see how you lived. It would surprise a few of them! What happens over there?' Nial pointed to a gateway in the north side of the big outer cashel.

'Just beyond the outer wall is a long enclosure where Bronach grows her herbs. They are quite remarkable for their healing properties, and she is most skilled in their use. Poor Bronach, she had occasion to make use of them herself a couple of years ago.'

'What happened?'

'Ach, and it was a horrid thing, but she is much recovered now, though not just as amusing as she used to be. One day she fell from the wall of the garden and cracked her head on a stone. When we heard her shout we ran at once, but even as we carried her to her hut over there—she and our potter are the only two women who live inside the monastery boundaries—her speech began to slow, and she could not think rightly. In only a little while she had completely lost consciousness, and was still, and we thought we had lost her. By God's goodness, right in our midst had come that very morning one who claimed to have previously cured several folk who suffered in just this way.'

'That was lucky!'

'Call it what you want, but you can imagine our astonishment when he called for a knife and some hot beeswax, and began to cut away a piece of skin from the top of poor Bronach's head! Then, before our very eyes he started to chip-chip away at the living bone! I tell you, it was a blessing for her that she did not know what was going on, for by this time she was all but dead, though her heart still thumped. Every so often he would smear some of the beeswax round the edges of the hole he was making, and it seemed to quell the blood which oozed slowly out of the bone itself. He worked quickly, yet somehow delicately, but when the point of the knife broke through the bone and into her head, a jet of blood squirted out with such force that it sprayed all over him, and spattered on to nearly all of us who were present. I really do not know why I had stayed. It made me feel quite ill, and I was not the only one. All of us here have at one time or another seen a lot of blood flow, for such are the ways of the world, but this was something—well, somehow different. I do not know what he did to her then, for I went outside, but those who could stay, said she opened her eyes within a moment of the flow easing.'

'Goodness!'

'Within seven days she was sitting up, and now, apart from a baldy patch where the skin grew again but without hair, she is well. The only thing is that she behaves a little oddly now and then, and in particular has developed a ridiculous and quite unaccountable hatred for red hair. Very awkward that is, sometimes. It is a good thing that yours is dark! Ach, and there she is, chatting to the guard at the side gateway! Come and meet her.'

Bronach was a tall, rather thin young woman with wispy brown hair and the sort of face that smiles out of sheer habit, and then every so often bursts into a dazzling grin. Producing one of these specially for Nial's benefit, she hitched the embroidered hem of her fawn cloak up on to her bony shoulder, and waved cheerfully.

'And isn't it himself!' she cried in a high, rather rattly sort of voice. 'Och, an' Lugh an' me were just talkin' about ye! But he gave me tae believe yez were a bit older than y'are by my eyes.' She turned on the guard with a giggle, stuck out a horny foot and flicked the shaft of his spear so that he had to make a wild grab to stop it falling. 'Y'oul' fool ye! Didn't I tell yez if he wasn't going to be borned for a long time yit, he was boun' to be young!' She glanced at Cailan and winked saucily. 'Aye, an' it just had to be the likes of you who foun' him! Always the one for the quare things, you are! Och well, sure he's a bonny lad even if he isn't really here at all at all at all.' She peered at Nial. 'Are ye?'

Nial felt embarrassed.

'I—think I am,' he said. 'But it does seem a bit unlikely, I know.'

'Naver you mind, boy! Just you enjoy it. It's always worth living. I know!' She grinned even more than before, and her wild eyes glinted with a look that made Nial feel just a mite afraid of her.

Bronach apparently sensed this, and suddenly slapped him heartily on the back with her bony hand, the strength of which shook him considerably.

'Ach! Naver be a-feared of Bronach, me boy! Sure, an' Cailan will tell ye, I never hurt a flea. Drat the things!' And she gave herself a good scratching all over. She smelled rather strongly, too, and Nial shifted round a little to his left so as to be less directly down wind of her. He was beginning to get used to, or not to mind so much, the somewhat unwashed state of those around him, but Bronach was overpowering! It was only when she suddenly ejected from her mouth a stream of bright-green liquid that he realised part of the stench was some herb or other that she was chewing. Her flickering eyes noted his change of expression.

'Herbs,' she croaked. 'This one's for me blood. But I can cure tooth-ache, boils, and fevers, och, an' a lot of other things besides. Me mother learned me about them. I can fix some headaches, too.' Her eyes narrowed. 'Yez haven't any warts, have ye?'

Nial hastily denied the existence of the one wart that he did possess and which he knew she couldn't see because he had that particular hand tucked into the cloth belt at the back of his tunic.

'Ach well,' sighed Bronach, 'come an' see me plants, anyway. Out of the road there, Lugh!' And once again the unfortunate guardian of the cashel found himself grabbing for his spear.

Through the massive outer wall ran a straight but narrow passage some fifteen feet long, which was the thickness of the wall at that point, and one had to duck under the great wooden beams over which the earthen rampart continued in its unhindered circle. As they emerged, there was a low wall of more ordinary proportions on their immediate right, joining another that ran straight across their path a few feet away, parallel to the great cashel. In the corner there, a few stones had been deliberately left projecting in such a way as to form steps so that one could more easily climb over, and so reach the open fields which lay beyond. Bronach sprang lightly up, but instead of continuing over, turned and jumped down into the enclosure on the right. Nial scrambled on to the wall himself, and saw that she was standing knee-deep in a dense collection of strange-looking greenery.

'That one's great when ye've over-ate,' she cackled, brushing the top of a scraggy plant with yellow flowers. 'An, there's one that fixes ye up when ye can't sleep. Here, smell!' And plucking the head off a plant she hove it at Nial with such accuracy that it would have hit him in the face if he hadn't moved quickly, though he nearly fell off the wall in his effort to catch it. Bronach chortled to herself, and continued her lecture on the properties of the various groups of this and that, some of which were purely spices, though most seemed to be used mainly for healing purposes. One in particular, a single-stemmed plant with pairs of biggish leaves and little rings of tiny white flowers growing out at different heights, was praised greatly. It stimulated and yet calmed one down, it killed pain and cleansed wounds, and above all, (this related with awe), it secured for the consumer the certainty of a long life! Not being at all interested in plants in the normal way, the only ones that Nial could recognise instantly were a cluster of different kinds of mint, and surprisingly, a little plot of dandelions growing in neat rows, and also a riot of brilliant orange flowers in the corner nearest him, against the great boulders of the cashel itself.

'Are those used for anything?'

'Saints bless ye, yes! Ye make a sort of paste with the leaves, to put on old scars, and it helps new skin to form. Look at me head!' And she bowed low in his direction, so that her hair fell forward to expose a bald patch that was stained bright yellow. 'As good as fixed, that is!' she cawed, and was pleased when Nial agreed. Then he pointed at the dandelions.

'What about those?'

'Ach well, apart from the young leaves bein' good eatin', if Cailan here was to get crotchety and start havin' spots on him, I'd give him a broth of them with a fair sprinklin' of these here thrown in and given a good rummle roun' when it boiled.' And she toed a low, tight-growing, bluey-green thing that immediately buzzed loudly and turned out to have been full of Cathal's bees. 'Naver known it fail to work,' and she glanced sideways at Cailan, 'have ye, me boy?'

7

The Battle of the Longship

It was late afternoon when Aengus and Finnian, somewhat shyly for all their advancing years, approached Nial and asked if, as a thin layer of cloud was slowly covering the sky and conditions would be just right, he would take them fishing in *Cuan*. Feeling extremely honoured, Nial agreed at once, but Cailan held up a slender hand and put his long fingers to Nial's mouth.

'What he means, Brothers, is that he will tomorrow; but today you and I are going to take him out in one of our skin boats.'

Nial pulled the hand away. 'No, really Cailan, I don't mind at all . . .' But Aengus shook his grey old head.

'My son, that is a grand idea! Why, I should have known better; only last night Cailan was telling me of the interest you had shown in our old boats. No, *you* shall come with *us*. You will be quite safe. My brother turned the big boat over a few days ago, but we will row, not sail, this time. Finnian! Have you got all the fishing things? The tide is already ebbing.'

Nial delightedly followed the two slight old men down past the cashel guards to the shore where the island boats were pulled up clear of the water, with Cailan trotting along behind him like a rather pleased dog. Over on the far side of the boulder 'quay', where he had not noticed them before, were two smaller skin boats lying upside down among the bracken.

'You will not mind if we use one of these,' said Aengus. 'I have not the strength of my youth any longer, and my brother has even less than I, after his disgraceful inversion last week. These are much easier to lift than the big craft.'

Nial was surprised just how light in fact they were, for though the one they chose must have been over fifteen feet in length, it felt as though he and Cailan could have managed it down to the water between them. The likeness to the West of Ireland curraghs which Nial had once seen on a motoring holiday to those parts was almost unbelievable, but with the exception that cow-hide instead of tarred canvas was used to cover framework, and the boat was pointed at both ends.

When he climbed aboard, he found her amazingly stable for all her barrel-like centre-section, but the amount of creaking and flexing that went on caused him some concern until he gradually got used to it. There was also considerable danger of putting a foot between the wicker ribs and through the stretched skin covering.

Under the persuasion of long slim-bladed oars held by leather thongs to wooden pegs driven into the gunwales, the high riding little boat spurted effortlessly forward. Only three oars were in use, for the white-haired Finnian was preparing the hand-lines in the stern while his brother at the stroke oar sang a swinging sea-song, leaving out certain words here and there because he was now a monk. Nial nevertheless caught the full sense of the ballad, and laughed till he could hardly row. Cailan, with his oar out on the other side, every so often called over his shoulder to Nial not to pull so erratically, for the double power on the port side kept swinging them out towards the middle of the lough, and it seemed they were bound along the shore of the island, to where the current ran strongly over a shoal and the fishing was particularly good.

With the oars inboard and the boat drifting into position over what Nial knew as the Rig Pladdy, Aengus, who was showing him how to attach the beautiful little bone hooks to the twine, suddenly paused and slowly straightened up.

'Cailan.' The voice was steady.

'Aye?'

'What do you make of that?'

The others followed the old man's gaze, but at first Nial could see nothing other than the long low humpy outline of the far shore, and its even lower off-lying islands, green and yellow in the evening light. Then he spotted the dark curved outline of the unmistakable prow of a longship, and the stubby tapering mast which stuck up in menacing stillness beyond the narrow spit that ran out from the end of one of the higher islands to the north.

'And where, by the Saints, did they come from?' Cailan sat bolt upright and as alert as a startled rabbit.

'That is mystery enough,' muttered Finnian in his rumbling, seldom-used voice. 'But I would not mind knowing just what they might be doing on Lang-ey.'

Nial felt a sudden tingle of excitement surging through him.

'Isn't that where Abbot Thol-whatever-his-name-was, had his treasure buried?'

Finnian held up a finger before his lips. 'Just so, my son, just so.' The glittering eyes narrowed in their deep, wrinkly hollows. 'Brothers, I think this might be worth a closer look.'

'We cannot,' said Cailan quickly, but with more than a hint of regret in his tone. 'We must not risk such trouble.'

'What has got into you?' Aengus turned to him. 'You are usually more ready to dare than most of us. Is not the knowledge of what they are doing worth something of a risk? If they discover their treasure has gone, there will be more than just a risk of trouble at Aendrum, for it is certain they will know all about our late Abbot, and how he deserted them for us, and him one of the few with knowledge of the treasure! Believe me, it is to Aendrum they will come to regain their loot. And you know their methods as well as I do. It is surely worth taking considerable chances to find out if indeed it is the treasure that they are looking for on Lang-ey?'

'No, Aengus, and I am sorry. But I cannot let anything happen to Nial.'

'Oh, Cailan!' Nial was appalled at the thought that it was he who should be the cause of turning back from such an adventure. 'Nonsense! I won't have that at all! I'm perfectly capable of taking care of myself, and—well, just think how I would feel if they did raid the monastery and no one knew they were coming and we all got murdered in our beds!'

'I still think we should put you ashore on our island first.'

'No! Look, if—*if*—there was any trouble, as you put it, I could—well,' he cleared his throat, 'we of the twentieth century have one or two tricks that, er, that you wouldn't know about. Really, I'll be all right.'

Cailan sighed and nodded. 'I hope you are correct. They are wily enemies, and oh, by the Saints, they are hard to love, sometimes! Well, Brothers, and how shall we get close enough to see what is going on, without being chased?'

'That,' rumbled Finnian, dropping his baited line over the side and apparently settling himself comfortably on the thwart, 'that will not be difficult, so long as we do not *seem* to be watching; say, just following a shoal of fish, with, er, two of us rowing and the other two making a reasonably good number of catches.'

'The first part is grand, for Nial and I can row.' Cailan swung his oar into position and looped the thong over the thole-pin.

'But, good fishermen as you and Aengus are, how can you know you'll be catching *any* fish, let alone a "reasonable number"?'

'We only need two or three—ah! Here is the first! If we—catch it, Aengus!—Thank you, if we keep putting them back in, still on the line, and hauling them out again, I am sure we could look as though we were having considerable luck.'

Cailan grinned, and helped Nial prepare his oar. 'Tut, tut, Brother! Not exactly honest, is it?'

'The fish will not mind at all. Look!' And he hit the silvery mackerel a terrific 'thwack' against the gunwale. 'This one is quite dead!'

Instead of making directly for Lang-ey, Nial and Cailan pulled the swift little boat on a more easterly course, so that before long they were hidden from sight behind a number of pladdies, the weed-covered boulder tops of which had already dried quite a few feet clear of the falling tide. There they were able to put on a spurt and head rapidly up to a small islet. Beaching the boat briefly on its lee side, Cailan jumped ashore and scrambled up the stony mound to lie among the stiff sea-grass, where he could see Lang-ey from a distance of just over half a mile.

While they waited for him, Aengus turned to Nial and smiled.

'It was the work of God in Cailan that we did not, after all, come fishing in your boat, my son. She would have been far too conspicuous for this sort of thing, what with her brilliant paint and strange shape! Ah, good! Here he comes.'

Slithering down the brown weed, Cailan gave the boat a hefty shove and jumped aboard, but he did not take his place at the oar at once. Sitting almost casually on the raised bow with a foot still dangling overside in the water, he looked from one to the other of them as though making a calculation. Then he settled more comfortably on to the low seat.

'They are looking for the treasure. I am quite sure of it. Nothing else would have them digging and poking about like that, without even leaving anyone in charge of the longship—which appears to be at anchor close in under the high land on this side. They are working in a long line, gradually beating and prodding their way across to the other side. They obviously do not know the exact place to dig. But, you know, what puzzles me is why they should suddenly come looking for it, like this, all these long years after it was buried. Why, it is nearly two generations ago!'

Finnian ran a wet finger down the greenish back of the fish in his left hand, and nodded. 'It really does look as though that is what they are after. But when you think of it, perhaps it is not so strange that they should only come seeking it now. The story has it that they were all very drunk in that returning ship, and only Tholrykr and one other did the actual burying, and we know that after that they were fighting. Well, is it not just possible that only one of the ultimate survivors of that trip, perhaps then a young lad, was sober enough to remember where in the darkness of that dreadful night the burying had taken place?'

'Or even that it had taken place at all; I see your point, Finnian.' The sharp seaman's eyes of Aengus glinted with a liveliness they had not shown since he quit the sea, years before. 'I suppose such a youth could have lived on, keeping quiet about the treasure. If his health held him well, he could have died recently, telling his secret.'

Nial turned excitedly, rocking the curragh. 'This would explain what the longship was doing yesterday! If they had been given rather complicated directions as to how to find the right island—maybe the old man himself hadn't been quite sure—they could well have been piecing together the information; maybe counting so many islands before turning left, or something.'

'The boy is right! Bother!' Finnian thumped his hand with his fist, quite forgetting the fish, which squashed rather unpleasantly. 'Yes! That explains quite a lot of the apparently aimless little cruises we have recently watched from the Bell House! So! Now what do we do? They are bound to find it at any moment, and I really do not imagine there can be much of it left, for though the good Abbot used some of it for us, he is also known to have given considerable riches away to—well, Drumbo for a start, and we all have seen the jewelled bookshrine used by the monks at Commar at the head of the lough, not to mention all the things Aed has made out of it!'

Cailan began swinging the head of the boat round with his oar.

'There is only one thing we can do. Warn our people at Aendrum and try to get the islanders organised to defend themselves and us! Come, Nial! Pull hard!' But Finnian almost stood up in his sudden moment of inspiration.

'No, wait! I think we can gain at least an evening—perhaps the night as well!'

'If only we could!' Aengus glanced keenly at him.

'But we can! At least, if we have God with us, we can. Did not Cailan say their longship was anchored on this side of the island, and that they were all working their way over to the far side? If—if we could just get to it without being seen—well, Cailan and Nial know enough to help us quite a bit, Aengus. If we could get the ship away and maroon them on the island . . .'

'No good, Finnian. They would walk ashore at low tide, and it will be that not long from now. Though, when I think of it, it might take a good enough time for them to find boats in which to get back to their homes, and even longer to walk down to the Narrows if they failed. What think you, Cailan?'

But Cailan shook his head. 'We would never do it without being noticed. One of them would be sure to look up. Besides, the four of us could never row a longship any distance, and if we were to attempt such a thing at all, we would simply have to get clear away out of their swimming range.'

'Who said anything about rowing?' said Nial urgently. 'Why everything's as right as it could be for sailing her out! We just cut the anchor warp, set the sail—surely we could swig that up between us—and with the wind where it is it would almost be a dead run out between this little island and Lang-ey! What could go wrong with that?'

'Quite a lot, if we let it,' said Aengus, though grinning at the prospect. 'We quite often fish hereabouts, my brother and I, and there is a very long spit running out under water, and also a nasty shoal that you cannot see at all, except at low water. Even the other side of this near islet is shallow and dotted with boulders for a long way out towards the shoal. No,' and for just a moment Nial thought he was going to disagree, 'no, we will just have to do it right the first time. Now, what about getting there to start with? We must not be heard, and if by ill chance we are seen, we must at least look as though we were still merely fishing.'

'I know!' exclaimed Nial. 'Could we possibly look less like monks? I mean, well, if they did see us getting away, and we looked, well, more like the local fishermen, then they wouldn't necessarily head straight for the monastery whenever they do find transport.'

'That too, is dishonest.' Cailan prodded his back. 'But an excellent idea! If we take our brown robes off, that should help.'

'I hope we will not make trouble for innocent people,' mumbled Finnian, pulling not only his cloak over his head, but his tunic as well, exposing his skin-and-bones old body to the breeze which now blew more freshly from the north-east. 'There! Now, if I tie my cloak sideways round my waist—like this—and Aengus wore just his tunic, maybe Cailan could go without, and, er, . . .'

'I've got it!' Nial took off his own tunic, and still making use of the cloth belt to hold it, folded the garment flat and wrapped it round his waist like a big bath-towel. He also kicked off his sailing shoes. 'Now we all look different, and thoroughly uncivilised. But won't you be awfully cold like that, Cailan? Couldn't you at least do like Dichu, and wear your tunic as a sort of white cloak?' In fact, Nial noticed again how warm the breeze was, even though the sky was by now quite darkly overcast.

'I could indeed,' said Cailan, and handed Nial the little bronze brooch. 'Here, look after this for me, please. Go on! It will be safe enough if you tuck it into a fold of the tunic—yes, there! That is fine!'

So it was indeed a very 'local' looking boat that came fishing its way leisurely out from behind the islet, and across the short gap between it and the next drying shoal near the land, its shabby-looking crew dividing their attention only between the oars and the fish which they were hauling into the curragh with such remarkable dexterity. Cailan and Finnian, in an anguish of curiosity, firmly kept their heads turned away from the big island, but Nial and Aengus took many cautious stares at the few Danes they could still see on its skyline. These were busily working away with sharpened sticks and even their swords, slashing at grass and bracken, and digging great sods of earth up here and there, but all the time moving further over the brow of the hill. Soon they would be lost to view behind it. A bigger problem was going to be the five or six who were down on the grassy-topped spit that ran out to the left, because this was virtually flat by comparison with the thirty-foot height of the more northerly part of the island; they would hardly disappear so conveniently.

As the boat slid in behind the low pladdy that was to be their last shelter from the gaze of the Danes should they choose to look, Nial and Cailan back-watered to take all way off, and they lay there quietly, maintaining their position against the breeze while Finnian and Aengus carefully stood up to see over the reef. By now only the heads of those on the high part of the island could be seen, but those on the spit were in full view. Not three minutes' row away from the curragh, and lying like a great brown swan on the ruffled grey water close under the shore, was the longship, her tall stem curving up to end in a fine spiral. They could see the red and white stripes of her sail hauled in a casual stow over its lowered yard. And they knew they dared not approach her.

Suddenly a great shout went up on the far side of the island, and with a cheering whoop, the Danes on the spit turned and ran towards the high part, while up there the remaining heads and shoulders vanished from sight with equal verve.

'Come on!' yelled Aengus, sitting himself on a thwart and grabbing an oar. 'If we go now, we'll do it!'

'I take it—' puffed Cailan between strokes, as they shot out from behind the shoal, 'that they have found—it?'

'Think so!' gasped Finnian, with some surprisingly active muscles rippling in his elderly back. 'But they're all—over the other side. If—they would just—stay there long enough—'

With a bubbling wake hissing out astern, and the force of the oars leaving swirling circles in the water, they drove the creaking, bending craft until Nial heard the blood beginning to pound in his ears, and felt the blade weighing more and more each time he lifted it from the water. He plunged it forwards and in and lay back at full stretch, and as his legs and back sprang tight with the effort, felt the boat lift swiftly onwards. Though Aengus and Finnian frequently glanced over their shoulders and by pulling harder than ever, or a bit less so, made slight corrections to the course, he himself did not dare look round, for fear partly of losing time and getting rammed in the back by Cailan, who somehow had a very much longer reach than he could achieve, and partly of seeing the Danes reappearing over the hilltop.

Finnian suddenly sprang up and with the brown robe swinging about him, he spun round and began to use his oar over the stern, steering the boat in a shallow curve to the left. Nial felt Cailan also cease to row and begin to prepare the bow line, the oar trailing from its leather thong.

'Easy!' Finnian's voice had a strength of tone not heard for many a year, and Aengus and Nial swung their oars inboard. There was a slight jolt, and Nial found himself staring at the wide planks of the longship's side. Cailan was aboard it in a flash, and taking a quick turn of the rope around a convenient hook just inside the massive oak rail, he started forward. In a second the others leapt over on to the solid deck, only to see him backing towards them away from the prone figure of a Dane who was at that moment waking from a snatched sleep under a rack of spare oars. With the single thought in his mind that if the man raised the alarm the whole scheme would go horribly wrong, Nial launched himself forward, seized one of the heavy oars from its place and swung it with all his might in the direction of the rising figure. The Dane let fly a terrific bellow of rage, but it was cut short by the thud of the oar on the side of his neck, followed by the 'clunk' of his nead hitting the end support of the rack, and finally he produced a sort of gurgling choke and lay still on his side on the deck.

Finnian sprinted with astonishing agility up the long centre gangway that ran over the top of the rowing thwarts to the bows, and through which were stepped the thick mast and supports for the lowered sail and spare oars. The others followed to the foot of the mast and began sorting out which of the coarse ropes hanging from it was the halyard, As Finnian shouted 'All clear!' and threw the untied end of the anchor warp overboard, they looked up, and there, staring down at them in utter disbelief from the top of the island was a stocky figure, bare to the waist and holding a sword in one hand.

'Hee-Ya!' The cry came sharply down and rang over the water.

'Come on!' gasped Cailan, swinging on a rope. 'It's this one!'
'Hee Ya-Ho!'
They put their combined weight on the halyard and with the folds of canvas falling from the yard, the latter began to sway upwards. Finnian, whose brown girdle seemed to have fallen by the wayside, pattered thinly by like a flitting shadow on his way aft. The steering oar thumped lazily against her rounded quarter as the great boat began to drift astern in the breeze. Almost dangling from the hairy rope in their efforts to make sail, Nial and Cailan were too engrossed in what they were doing to see the sight of some fourteen furious young Danes racing down the hillside in great leaps and surges towards them. Aengus saw them, and hove even harder, so that the yard came up against the sheave, and they had to ease it an inch or so before making fast, to prevent it from jamming. The huge striped sail thundered and clapped in the wind, and with no time to catch their breath, Aengus hustled Nial and Cailan aft to the sheets

and braces with a few crisp orders that left no doubt in their minds as to what to do. Finnian was putting all his supple strength on the arm of the steering oar, and the stern was at last responding in a great slow curve towards the shore. He knew from the noise of splashes and shouts that the Danes were already beginning to swim out towards them, and that if the sail didn't fill, it would only be a moment before the first of them were clambering over the rail.

Nial felt the rope which he and Cailan were hauling on suddenly leap and tighten against them as with a final patter and thud the great sail became still, straining full of wind. He glanced back, and to his horror saw a bronzed and sinewy hand reach up and clutch the rail. Cailan moved first, picking up an oar and bringing the loom of it, where it was some two and a half inches thick, hard down on the invading fingers. There was a yelp and a splash. A cry from Finnian. Cailan prodded over the side, and the steering oar kicked and freed again in Finnian's grip. Cailan's oar was now being held onto, so he let it go, and it disappeared over the stern very suddenly. He got another one from the rack and winked as he passed Nial. 'Love your enemies! I always did love watching people swim! And there is nothing that I recall about bruising fingers; heels, yes; but not—' and he brought the oar down on another swarthy hand, 'fingers!'

'She's answering!' Finnian shouted in most unseamanlike excitement. 'She's coming round!'

Heeling quite a lot now in the still freshening wind, the longship was picking up speed and those in the water could no longer keep pace. Finnian and his crew however had completely forgotten about their curragh towing alongside, and lying low in it, getting their breath back, were three wet, bedraggled and very angry Danes. They bounded over the rail together, just as

Cailan, Nial and Aengus were joyously trimming the straining sail to better advantage, and only Finnian saw them coming. He gave a cry, but it was as well that Nial did not look round in time to see the mess made by the short, straight-bladed Viking sword that struck the old man's face, sending his thin pink body slithering over to redden the foaming wake. Aengus swung round, seized an oar that rolled loose on the deck. Like a blunt lance he drove it with all the vicious violence of white rage deep into the stomach of one of the other two Danes springing towards him down the deck. Eyes widening, the burly figure gasped, dropped a jagged-looking dagger, staggered backwards and doubled up over the rail, clutching at his abdomen. Nial, dodging the lunging tackle of the third man as deftly as though he was back on the school playing field, threw himself forward and got the knife. The first Dane stood hauling on the steering oar, his feet braced on the slanting deck as he swung the heavy boat round into the wind, his sword stuck redly in the rail beside him. Nial never thought, but launched himself at the man's side, dagger foremost. The Dane's leather-bound forearm deflected the blow so that Nial merely crashed into his target, the knife curving gracefully overboard. Aengus saw the short sword being plucked from the splintered oak and lifted high. His oar swung again. The Dane staggered; the sword flew from the jolted hand. Nial felt the man's weight crumple fully on him, and expecting the searing pain of a wound as he was, it was a second or two before he realised the strong-smelling fighter was no longer fighting, and he wriggled himself free.

Cailan and the remaining Dane were tumbling about the narrow centre-deck in a tangle of bare limbs, cloth and sheepskin, and rolled over the edge to fall with breathless grunts out of sight between the rowing thwarts. Nial tore after them to help, but on reaching the break in the deck found Cailan slowly getting off his attacker, whose head was twisted back almost under the shoulder. Cailan, his lips pursed and brow furrowed, gazed, breathing heavily, down at the lifeless body, and then looked slowly up at Nial. Overhead the red and white panels of the sail seemed suddenly to dance and blend as the ship swung round out of control, and the thunder of flogging canvas shook the massive mast until even the very hull itself began to shudder.

'The helm, quick!' Nial jumped up on a thwart and aft along the decking.

The aged Aengus lay on his back in a spreading pool of blood that dripped from his reddening tunic and trickled slowly down the slope of the deck. The sword—the same sword that had been jerked from the Viking as Aengus had struck with the oar—was almost up to its hilt in his right side, just below the ribs. Its crimson point had splintered the deck where he fell.

'Aengus! Oh, Cailan!' Nial threw himself on his knees beside the old man. 'Cailan! Come quick!' The silvery-haired head moved slightly. 'He's still alive!' Nial felt Cailan kneel beside him, saw Aengus open his eyes and the colourless lips move.

'G-good.' Aengus swallowed hard, choked a little, and swallowed again. 'Both—safe. Warn Aendr . . .' And a gush of blood from his mouth smothered the remains of his last word. Above, against the darkening clouds, the sail of its own accord stopped clattering, and formed once more into silent, rounded curves. The ancient words of Cailan's prayer sounded clearly in the sudden hush. The longship had fallen back on to the same tack, and again began heeling over and gathering headway.

It was Nial who saw the reef, right ahead and barely two boat-lengths away. He jumped to the swinging oar and struggled desperately with its projecting arm, but he had never handled such a thing before, and precious seconds flew by before he got the blade to grip the water firmly in the right direction. For what seemed like an age while the reef appeared to rush in under the proud sweep of the great stem-post, she failed completely to answer her helm. Then at last she commenced to bear away. A sudden squall howled into the bellying sail, heeling her further and further until Nial, still forcing the oar hard over, could see spouts of water jetting up through the rowlock-holes on the lee side. In a smother of foam the curragh broke adrift and spun bobbing away in the wake. A stack of oars came clattering down from the rack. The brown weed was all about them now. It was not with any surprise that Nial felt the deck tremble, heave and cant over under his feet. The great mast snapped, and for a moment, ropes, blocks and sail rattled and thrashed about him. Then there was silence. Stillness ...

'I suppose I had better put my tunic on properly.' Cailan's voice was calm, almost casual.

'Huh?'

'Our only hope of escape now is to wade ashore and get round the top of the lough—*if* the Danes do not cut us off. It will be a long journey in the dark.'

'You mean ...' Nial was puzzled, baffled by the sudden turn of events.

'I mean come on! Peace to you, Mo-Nial.'

'But what about—' Nial looked at the blood-smeared bundle that had been the old monk.

'Aengus is all right. *That* is dead.'

In a daze, Nial followed over the rail and into the weed-cluttered water. It felt chill round his thighs as he struggled to keep his feet among the hidden stones. Cailan, pulling his sodden tunic over his head, stumbled and went in, but it didn't matter.

They had quite a lot of deep wading to do when they reached the far side of the reef and crossed the wide gap of wind-ruffled water between there and the nearest point of the next island. At one place it proved quicker to swim for a few yards. In the distance they could see the Danes doing precisely the same thing, except that they had only the one space to cross.

The island that Nial and Cailan now found themselves on was only just separated from its neighbour at high water. The muddy gap between that one and the mainland turned out to be even smaller. Nial paused, and started to untie the water-soaked knot of his woven belt. He might as well be properly dressed for this. It was clearly inevitable now that they *would* be caught. Even if instead of coming ashore they had tried to hide, it could hardly have helped. The Danes were already coming across to find them.

There was no point in heroics. Cailan wasn't going to fight, he could see that at a glance. You cannot defend yourself physically when you're down on your knees praying. It all seemed so pathetic, so wasteful.

Suddenly his fingers felt the hardness of the little brooch pinned in his tunic. He looked at the bowed head at his side—and quickly struggled into the garment, keeping the brooch inside it. He didn't want to be captured naked. As he hastily re-knotted the belt round his middle he realised that he didn't want to be captured at all, and in a brief flash of anger he glanced round for a weapon. A stick, or anything—but there was nothing. He wondered what it was like to die, what Aengus and the others had felt back there on the longship.

Six of the Danes had now splashed across, wet and mud-covered like himself. For a moment they halted, staring at Nial and his silent companion. A thick-set, red-headed youth, standing with his feet apart and his arms folded, smiled slowly, greasily, and said something. The words were Norse.

Nial stood still, his heart banging furiously. But there was no point in moving. Some instinct suddenly told him it might be all right—that he wouldn't be killed—not here—not for the moment.

The Danish youth nodded to his companions. They came forward in a bunch. One of them removed a leather belt from his sturdy waist. Nial braced himself, somehow knowing that to hit out would be asking for death. They grabbed him, forced his arms behind him and bound his wrists tightly together with the belt. Cailan was given the same treatment, and looked peculiarly grateful.

Roughly, they were hustled over the mud and on to join the rest of the longship's ex-crew. So far as Nial could judge, every one of them was young—not much older than himself. They were mostly swarthy and dark, but the occasional fair head stood out amongst them. They all had short swords or strange-looking axes, and their clothes were as brief and bedraggled as his own, though they all wore sandal-like leather shoes, well laced on. These gave them a great advantage during that dark and wearying night's march down the east coast of the lough. Mostly they followed the shore, stumbling along interminably over the dark stones and broken shells. Nial knew his feet were cut, but likewise knew that no one would be interested. He could occasionally feel the blood going sticky between his toes, but he dared not stop. He had tried that once, and was actually cut by the swordpoint that ushered him on. Not a bad cut, but enough to keep him going long after he felt like dropping. Then they were led inland somewhat, and the going became softer. Grass and bracken; thistles. Once or twice there would be the smell of smoke in the air, and a dog would bark, but they saw no one. Only once did everyone stop briefly to drink at a small, cold streamlet, deeply refreshing.

Sometime just before the icy grey light of dawn flooded gradually into the sky on their left, Cailan tripped and fell, doing something horrible to one ankle. For a time he could only hop along, then he was able to hobble, and finally limp. As the light spread, Nial could see that the ankle was badly swollen, and he was amazed that Cailan could use it at all.

They stumped on up a rise, and suddenly the sun broke the horizon, unexpectedly almost behind them, glinting faintly on the far-distant Irish Sea. The tired group now turned right among densely growing trees, clambering over dead branches and past thickets of brambles, down once more to the terrible stones of the lough shore. Ahead of him, through heavy eyes, Nial saw the unmistakable inlet now known as Audley's Roads, and further round to the left, across the swirling silver of the ebb tide forcing through the Narrows, several columns of blue wood-smoke rose into the crisp morning air. 'Don't go anywhere near the Narrows,' his father had said, and at that minute Nial would have given a lot to be able to obey, for he knew that over there lay the Danes' own settlement.

8

Boyhood Hide-hole

There was a good deal of shouting by those around him before they managed to attract attention from the opposite shore, but eventually a boat put out, pulled by four old men who worked their way well uptide before making any attempt to cross over. To Nial's surprise, when everyone had piled in so that the stout little craft lay deep and heavy in the water, not one of the youngsters gave a hand with the rowing. For him, and no doubt even more so for Cailan, the bliss of being allowed to sit down and ease the pain in his legs was such a relief that he paid little enough attention to the way the boat was twisted this way and that on the journey back across the boiling current. The only moment of interest was when someone produced a length of rope and tied it round his neck, taking the other end round Cailan's neck in the same way, so that their heads were held less than two feet apart. Even at that, the trip was sheer luxury in comparison to that of the past five hours. It seemed no time at all before the nose of the boat was being run up the stony shore behind the little islet off Strangford village. And what a strange village it was.

A large number of wooden buildings were perched round the creek, some of them low and very long with turf roofs. More straggled on the hills behind, but it was towards a single stone-built one that Nial and Cailan found themselves being pulled, stiff after being so still in the bottom of the boat, and feeling awkward with their necks tied so closely together. Groups of scruffy, ragged children ran towards them, dancing and shouting what could only be insults, and spitting at them.

They were dragged round the side of the building away from the water. A sudden pebbly slope led downwards through a narrow gap in the solid rock on which the house was constructed. A heavy door led into some sort of cellar that stank of rotten fish and far worse, and there they were left among the darkness and loud buzzing of countless flies. The door was wedged firmly shut behind them.

It was not actually completely dark, for gradually their eyes became accommodated to the few cracks of light that found a way round the well fitted door. Cailan was still gasping from the pain of his ankle.

'Those last few paces undid all the good done resting it in the boat! Ach! What dirty people these are! It is not too pleasant here, is it? But look! That is surely a wooden floor above us! I wonder if we can find a way out?'

'We certainly won't shift this door,' puffed Nial, having just tried. 'I say, Cailan; we really are in a mess, aren't we!'

'Ach, it is not too bad, if you do not stand where I just put my foot.'

Despite himself, Nial chuckled. It was good to have someone with him who could, after all that had happened, still crack some sort of a joke.

'Nial,' Cailan's fingers found and gripped his wrist, their elbows rubbing together. 'Do not fear! I have asked for help, so that we might yet manage to warn the Abbot before it is too late. And there is something else in our favour.'

'What? It seems to me that everything has gone just about as wrong as it possibly could! Look, turn round a bit further. I think I could undo your thongs!'

'No. It will be better if you do not. They will come again,

and would only tie us up more permanently. Be content as you are until help comes.'

'That may be too late.'

'Not if you share my faith, Mo-Nial. Help *will* come. Besides, we have yet to see those twentieth century tricks you spoke of in the curragh.'

'What? Oh, for goodness sake! I only *said* that. I—I—' he felt terrible, 'I'm afraid it was a lie.'

Cailan paused, but only for a second. 'Well, never mind. You are still alive! That in itself means that you will yet have the chance to carry out your Purpose.'

'Och, Cailan!' Tears of frustration suddenly began to spurt into Nial's eyes. 'How many times do I have to say that I know of no such "Purpose"! You persist in thinking that I am some sort of a prophet or something! Well I'm not, I tell you! I'm NOT! I know only that by some twist of time I have come out of the twentieth century and landed in the same place a thousand years earlier. I know nothing of your period, your people, or your ways! Why I can speak your language with such ease is as beyond me as the rest of it. If you want to pray, you can pray me back into my own time! I can forecast nothing, except that your—' He paused, biting his lip hard.

'Yes, Nial?'

'Nothing.'

'It might be important to us.'

'It isn't. At least—oh, God, I hope not!'

'Ahem! Tell me, though.'

'All right, then! I have hinted at it before. Nendrum—Aendrum, as you call it, and everything built there, is to be destroyed; I think by the Danes, and I think now. It seems to me they have good enough reason for it! All, even the church and the round tower—Bell House as you call it—the school, everything will be left in ruins. I *know*, Cailan. As you once guessed, I have seen those very ruins myself. *You* would not recognise them.'

The outburst was brutal, and effective. He felt awful.

Cailan was silent. Even the faint sounds of the settlement outside seemed to quieten. Then the grip on Nial's wrist tightened as above them the floorboards creaked and thumped to the pressure of hurried footsteps, and excited voices could be heard, rising in volume and then suddenly dying away. Then there was a lone voice, not over-strong, which seemed to be asking questions and getting a single, youthfully urgent string of words in reply.

Staring upwards in the smelly near-darkness, Cailan had his head as characteristically over on one side as the rope would allow. 'It is the crew of the longship,' he whispered.

'Can you understand them? Is that our young red-head?'

'Yes! Shh!'

Some more from the older voice, and then a series of emphatic tones from the young one.

'I think—if only he would go slower—but from a word here and there—they seem to be telling someone, maybe Cedric Fairhead, their leader, how they found the treasure—and—how there was not as much as they had been told. By the Saints! I believe the older man is *not* the leader, but his old cousin Eric, er, Haroldsson, I think he is—he is calling the young red-headed one his grandson. It seems it is Haroldsson who knows just how much treasure there *should* be! There is— much gone! It was not only—shh! They are having to explain why they walked back—listen!' A roar of derision greeted some statement by the young man, and he could be heard shouting indignantly in his defence. Then a hush fell, and a new voice spoke. The younger one replied slowly, as though describing something, and then a few words came in a rush.

'What's going on, for heaven's sake?'

'I hope Heaven hears for *our* sakes, Nial! I think he has just described us, and mentioned Tholrykr, too!' Even Nial heard *that*, so clearly was it spat out. A low murmur came from directly over them and footsteps thumped by and passed. There was silence.

To their horror the door behind them was flung open, and two bulky Danes stood in the bright space, the strong light outlining their fair hair and dirty grey fleece clothing. One of them held a sword. He barked something at them. Cailan glanced at Nial and gave him a rather thin smile.

'Peace to you, Nial.'

They stumbled out into the clean air and up the slope into the blinding sun. Nial could feel the cold iron blade against his upper arm as the Dane steered them back round to the main door of the heavily thatched building. It made his whole flesh creep.

Inside the longhouse it was cool and dim, and they were greeted by shouts and angry gestures from the tousled group of young warriors who had earlier captured them. Nial thought he was about to be lynched and went tense, but there came a gruff shout above the hubbub, and way was made for them up the centre of the long room, to where a wrinkled, grey-haired, ill-looking man rested back on a massive sort of throne that stood on a low wooden platform. As all the remaining floor was of clay and stone, it was obviously this portion that covered the prison. The thin legs of the old man were cross-gartered to above the knee, and he wore a brown tunic richly embroidered in black round the edges. Cold, steel-blue eyes peered out from his sunken, whiskered face. He looked from

Cailan to Nial. Nial's heart pounded painfully. The blood thundered in his ears.

One after another, strangely intoned questions were thrown at them. Nial caught only the words 'Lang-ey' and 'Veeking'; the rest meant nothing. He glanced sideways at Cailan, who didn't seem to follow it either. The old man raised an infuriated fist and thumped it down on the arm of the heavy chair. The hand was like a claw; its three middle fingers were missing.

Six men came forward—men! They looked like men, and behaved like adults in their bearing, but their faces and blustering self-important manners showed them to be far younger. They began a long dissertation, presumably on how they had taken the two prisoners after the longship had stranded.

The old one seemed hardly to be listening; instead he was staring fixedly at Cailan's face, and fingering his own wispy beard. He spat out a word, and everyone turned and gazed again at the pair of them. Nial saw Cailan's expression tighten a fraction, and his head turn a little to one side, but the blue eyes never left the old man's face. On their left there was a cry of rage and the red-haired youngster darted forward and started bellowing at the old man. Nial, recognising the urgent, exaggerated tones, felt the back of his neck beginning to prickle, and he flinched suddenly as the blade of a sword flashed upwards past his ear. The old man held up his tattered paw, and only the youngster was left shouting.

Eric Haroldsson rose from the great chair and towered over his hot-headed grandson. The youth fell silent, sullenly. Nial shuddered as the cold iron point of the sword was lowered on to his shoulder, where it twitched restlessly. He took a deep breath and held it, but all was well. The elderly giant, who was more than a foot taller than the average of those crowded around him, stood upright and firm for all his sick looks; and speaking rapidly, was clearly giving the lad a good dressing down. Again Nial heard the word 'Veeking', and again there was a deep-throated titter of laughter from behind him. The sword vanished from his shoulder, but he dared not look round.

Vainly the red-head urged some move or other, brandishing a broad sort of dagger now, but a shout from the gaunt figure silenced him, and was followed by a tediously made remark that had Cailan relaxing considerably, though only noticeably to someone as closely in contact as Nial. Then with a quick flurry of movement and a great cry the youth swung round on them, weapon raised, eyes wild with fury and injured pride. Monks! Sneering disdain was twisting his already unpleasant face. He made as though to strike at Cailan, but the latter's steady stare which shifted and met his own seemed to halt him in mid-swing. He faltered, and then lunged directly at Nial who found himself stumbling backwards to the floor, choking. The enraged youngster landed by his side and raised the dagger again, but the blade never landed! Almost sick with fright and gasping to get a breath, Nial saw the old man's claw clamp itself round the upraised wrist, and the other bony fist bang down on the knuckle part of the weapon-hand, so that the knife clattered across the floor. The rope round Nial's neck slackened now as Cailan bent his head carefully close, and with some contortion, managed to help him back to his feet. It was he who had first jerked Nial down.

The piercing eyes of Eric Haroldsson looked them over in turn, as if making a difficult decision. His maimed hand still held the wrist of his cursing grandchild, keeping the lad firmly down on the floor. He spoke, wearily, a distant expression on his whiskery, wizened face, and once more came the agonising wrenching of the neck-rope and the unmerciful dragging, as the two prisoners were tugged back to the door and pushed, stumbling, out into the sunshine. The wind seemed to have died, and the heat burnt into them comfortably. A momentary view of the harbour gave Nial a fleeting picture of remarkable beauty centred by a single longship lying alongside a small wooden jetty. The white line of her horizontally stowed sail slung low, reflected in the pale-blue water. A violent jerk on the neck-rope and the terrifying slap of a sword blade across his shoulders spun him on, down once more into the shade of the high rock and back to the stinking cellar. Here, further rope was produced. First his elbows were lashed painfully close behind him, putting even more strain on the belting round his wrists; but the tail of the rope was roughly, brutally passed down between his legs, thence between Cailan's and up round *his* elbows in the same way. As the door was being secured, (extra well, to judge from the banging which suggested props being wedged against it from the rock-face opposite,) they discovered this new arrangement enabled them to stand, and even sit, if they got down carefully, side by side, tight up against each other. It did not, however, enable them to get back-to-back where they might undo each other. Cailan moaned softly, and Nial asked if he was all right.

'In many ways, yes; but I am thinking some terribly un-Christian thoughts, I fear!'

'You saved my life up there, Cailan! I know it doesn't sound much, but I'm most awfully grateful!'

'That we are either of us alive is only by God's goodness.'

'God helps those who help themselves,' muttered Nial.

'What a remarkable truth! I must write that in my book when... Ach! Perhaps I will just remember it. *Nial*!' Forgetting himself, he turned excitedly, and the ropes bit into them both.

'Steady on!' gasped Nial.

'I—oh—I am sorry! But I must tell you! If we can survive here until night falls, and can then escape, we . . .'

'Don't be silly! How are we to get out with this lot round us?'

'Ach, listen, will you! That is not important! The thing is that if we *can* get away, we might have most of the next day before they can even think of attacking the monastery!'

'What? How do you make that out? I thought you couldn't understand them, up there?'

'Aye, unfortunately I cannot be completely sure, as I followed only a little of all that shouting, but I think they will not have enough longships until the rest of the fleet returns from—I *think* they said some celebration on Monanan, and that only *might* be tomorrow! The crews would maybe be tired, and as they would almost certainly attack in daylight, they would probably rest until . . .'

'There's only one ship in the harbour; I did notice that!'

'Well, from what I gathered, they reckon to need at least three more in order to outnumber the population of our island! They would know how many fighters we have as they have been collecting Scat from us for years.'

'Scat?'

'Aye. Everyone pays it in one form or another. It protects us from raids, they tell us. Very few people are Scat-free. Pay it, and all will be well. We have long doubted that, and now it seems we have been right.'

'Oh, I remember now. The Abbot told me about it. He was somewhat doubtful himself. Look Cailan, we simply must try and find a way out of this. Come on! Get up—ow! Carefully, now! There! Let's see if we can feel our way round. There may be some way, perhaps by going further in, or maybe up. After all, that is only a wooden floor above us. Maybe if no one was up there during the night, we might manage to prize a board up, or something. Let's see if there's a way! If only it wasn't so confounded dark!'

They did not get far.

Groping along the stonework to the right, they came on smooth, solid rock within a mere yard, and by the way that it curved sharply round, it seemed obvious they were in a very small 'cave' indeed.

'Ach,' muttered Cailan, a long while after they had settled down again, 'I wish they would bring us some food, for my middle really aches.' He sighed. 'But they will not. They do not feed prisoners, I understand.'

Nial shuddered, but hunger was tearing at his insides, too. 'No food at all?' His lips were dry. 'What about water?'

'I believe not. We were lucky at that stream, last night. There will probably be a rat or two later, though. If we could kill one, we might drink its blood.'

'You're joking. Aren't you?'

'Only a little, I admit. But I gather it has been done. Rats can be quite tender, I think.'

'I'd much rather you didn't. Do change the subject! Er, tell me more about what went on up above. You understood quite a lot really, didn't you?'

'Ach, but I can be sure of none of it, Nial. I wish I could. It is a difficult tongue to follow, for it sings in all the wrong places. Ranvaig once tried to teach me, but he gave up. But as far as I could make out, the old one, Eric Haroldsson, *if* that is who he is, has been left in charge while his cousin, Fairhead, and practically all the fully-fledged warriors are attending some festivity thing, having left only two longships and the handful of youths behind under Eric's orders.

'It looks as though the old one thought it would keep the boys out of mischief if he told them the yarn about the treasure, just as you guessed. It may have been he who was in Tholrykr's ship. I think he is angry that his own grandson—Lief Thorsson, someone called him—should be the one who had a precious longship stolen from under his feet. The fact that it was four mere monks who captured it—he recognised us as such, you must have seen—and that we then wrecked it, does not improve his wrath—with the boy, not us. It seemed to me that he felt you and I showed much courage and bravery in what we did. They almost worship bravery, you know. Sinful, but there you are! Indeed, I have heard that they sometimes give exceptionally brave prisoners a sword with which to defend themselves a bit at their execution, so that they will die fighting and thus go to "Valhalla". That is their idea of Heaven, I suppose. Ach, but I hope they do not give me a sword; I was never any good with one, and would make but a fool of myself! However Nial, they do hold bravery in great account, and we still have our lives, accordingly.'

Nial hitched himself up against the door a bit. 'Having heard what a blood-thirsty lot they were, I've been rather surprised about that,' he admitted. 'What happens now?'

'The boy was pressing for an immediate surprise attack on Aendrum, as a reprisal and in order to regain the treasure. However, the old man will not permit it until the rest of the ships come home. He is ill, though, and my greatest fear is that the lad and his nasty little friends will fill the remaining boat and attack anyway.'

'I thought you said there wouldn't be enough of them?'

'Not against *all* the islanders. But without our own warning, the Abbot will not know to get the farmers inside the cashels in time! On their own, the monastery might manage to repel the warriors themselves, but the losses would naturally be great because of the surprise it would be to them.' Cailan paused, and then went on, his voice low, 'For all our guards and lookouts, maybe *because* of them, Aendrum has not been seriously attacked for over a hundred years. I could not honestly say that more than a mere handful of us would have the least idea of what to do.'

For a time there was silence again, then Nial sought to break up the dismal train of thought.

'Cailan, are they really as bad as you make out? The Danes, I mean. What of the people who live hereabouts? They aren't all Danes, surely?'

'Not at all, ach no. But the Danes have made slaves of most of them. But maybe they are straight with them even then. I do hear the local folk have got so used to it that they hardly think of themselves that way. They seem to be well enough fed, if the few that I have met are anything to go by.'

'Must you mention food again?'

'Sorry!'

Utter stillness once more enveloped the dark cavern, and by and by, it became truly dark, for the sun's rays which earlier had lined up with the cracks in the heavy door and cast golden beams of floating dust into the gloom, no longer slanted that way. Nial dozed fitfully, exhausted after the terrible, sleepless night of marching and all the other excitements. He lost all sense of time. Once he woke to hear flies buzzing drowsily in the putrid air, and from outside a few distant shouts. The absence of any sounds of motor-transport or other machinery once more struck him forcefully as he waited in the silent darkness; waited, he knew not for what. His stomach rumbled painfully, feeling oddly tight. Despite himself, he thought of the chocolate and fruit, not to mention the tin of beans, all of which lay under the foredeck of his little *Cuan*. *Cuan*. An inanimate object which had come back through the ages with him, paint, sail, engine and all fresh as a daisy. He could make no sense of it at all. He probably wouldn't see her again, anyway.

The hours ticked by. Or were they only minutes? He wished he could see his watch. It was strange that he hadn't been robbed of it; and then it occurred to him that its metal bracelet, sprung internally, would probably look solid and permanent to these folk. Just as well, really.

Cailan made no sound, beyond that of deep, steady breathing, and was presumably asleep. In time, Nial fell asleep again himself.

There were small scuffling noises in the darkness, oddly distant, and yet in the cave. The wakening thought of rats sprang a cold prickle of sweat onto Nial's forehead.

They seemed to be mostly over to the left, for some reason. They maybe had food there. He hoped so. He didn't fancy being their next meal. He had once read how a group of them could attack . . .

His mouth felt dryer than ever and his lips were cracking, flaking, and he wanted desperately to waken Cailan, to know that everything was all right, to have comfort . . .

There was a sudden clatter of stones, and Cailan leapt violently against him and writhed up so that they both fell over in a tangled panic. Nial rolled to one side, the rope tightened on his throat, his eyes bulged with the pressure of it and for a moment his tongue seemed to fill his mouth completely, open though it was in the gasp of fright. He couldn't shout! By fortune, Cailan, in trying to rise, fell over him and the rope slackened. Nial lay panting and coughing, pain from the other rope searing his thigh. He could hear someone speak, but his ears were singing with induced sound, and he did not understand. Little flashes of light danced and burst in his brain. Half consciously he felt his elbows, then his wrists being tugged at. It was seconds before he realised that his hands were freed! He spread his arms out cautiously along the floor. What had happened? A hand came slapping over his face, stifling him. He felt the hairy forearm that pressed on his chest, and knew at once it wasn't Cailan's! Panic soared again within him and . . . 'Who's there?' . . . the words croaked past his clenched teeth as he struggled to get free.

'Shish, now! Shish, I say! Is Ranvaig! Stop fightings, or how do I untie your neck? Be shtill, now! And peace to you!'

'What?'

'Quiet, Nial, for pity's sake! It is Ranvaig come to help us!'

'Ranvaig!' Nial almost shouted the name.

'Shish, now Brother! You be quietly, please! Then come. I get you from here.'

Cailan's voice positively danced. 'May every saint bless you!'

'But in silent, please! Is many ears of Dane about.'

'Why ever did you not say it was you at first? I nearly strangled myself, and probably Nial too! Where are you?'

'Here. My pardons, Brother. But I am not knowing if some guard is by the door, so I have quietened me.'

'How in the world did you get in?' Nial stretched out his arms in an effort to locate the big monk.

'Is boyhood hide-hole. We live by here, once. Shetelig and me. Many years away, now. Shetelig find cave in hill some day. Air hole to here behind this big rock. Is small and old. We make it bigger. Are good games we play here! No one sees this hole without lamps, and no one brings here a lamp, as is sometimes prison. Come, I show you. Whereabouts Aengus and Finnian?'

It was Cailan who told him.

'Dead?' repeated Ranvaig softly. 'Ah, sad, sad. I feel you limp, Cailan!'

'It is no matter—ach! Listen!'

There were sudden thumps and clatters on the other side of the door.

'They're coming for us!' Nial's heart began thumping wildly, and when his groping hands found cloth, he gripped it hard.

'Is my arm you hold down, friend. Here, feel edge of hole! There! Go please.'

Nial didn't need any further instruction, and indeed found Cailan's bony frame practically scrambling over him as they fell through into the blackness of sharp tumbled rock. Even as Ranvaig climbed down beside them, they saw the flicker of torch-light outline the hole, and the shouts of surprise and fury which followed rang into the darkness beyond them. They felt Ranvaig grab them, hold them down in a crouch, and pull them away to the left. In a yard or two he stopped, found and pressed each firmly on the top of the head to indicate a low roof. Then he put Cailan's hand on Nial's shoulder and taking Nial by the wrist, he led on round an invisible curve to the right, feeling his way, but at a speed born of familiarity and great confidence.

They were splashing sightless through a deepening pool of icy water when they heard the shouting suddenly come louder again, and they knew their escape hole had been found. Ranvaig merely quickened his already incredible pace in the total obscurity of the low, meandering passage. Nial and Cailan bumped and scuttled along behind him as best they could, scrambling up and down unending, unseen slopes, over unexpected boulders and round bend after twist until Nial, still doubled over, had utterly lost his sense of direction. He had skinned an elbow on the rough wall, and could feel the warm blood trickling. He felt the grip on the shoulder of his tunic pull harder, and knew by the audible gasping that Cailan could not take much more of this. Round another corner. Clay under his feet. So this was what it was like if you were blind. Stones. Cailan was moaning piteously now, but still going. They could hear splashing behind them, but so far no light reached their part of the tunnel. Twist left. The strong hand on his wrist tugged him hard down now, and even at that his head banged painfully on some low projection. He felt weak and dizzy and every muscle ached. Cailan was stumbling. And then Ranvaig slowed all of a sudden and they collided heavily with him.

'Is yust here, somewhere. Ah! Must climb up high on you rights! Feel it? Up, then!' And standing behind them he helped them into a cavity of some kind about four feet above the downward-sloping floor. Once up, Nial felt all round him, groping hastily about on either hand, but could find no way out at all, and by the time Cailan was crouched beside him and Ranvaig had come up too, he was squeezed hard against the back of it and simply could not move. To his horror he saw the torch-light pick out the opposite wall of the passage, and then Ranvaig pressed them still harder back against the curved side of the recess and spread his dark brown cloak out over them. Even through the garment's close texture, Nial saw the darkness brighten to the approaching torch. He held his breath, despite the desperate need to puff and pant. The light grew to sudden brilliance! His heart banged, banged, banged. The stumbling group sped by, their swords scraping against the rock.

'Yust one lamp,' whispered Ranvaig. 'Is good. Now watch,' and he lowered the cloak. The dimming flicker played momentarily on the far wall. A distorted shadow bobbed past. Then there was a splash, a cry, and the light went out. Shouts and the sound of thrashing water echoed up the tunnel, mingling with the hearty chuckles of Ranvaig.

'I did that some day,' he said happily. 'Is very cold and all deep. Will keep they busy to find home again. Come now and stand! We go up more.' And to Nial's surprise there was full headroom above him, and quite a gymnastic feat required to swing himself up to where Ranvaig placed his hands. Getting Cailan up was hard work for he was too weak now to help much himself, and was terribly apologetic.

'Is not matter now,' whispered their bulky guide. 'Next part is creep on chest. Under big boulder to Shetelig.'

And under big boulder to Shetelig it was.

9

Race to Give Warning

Ranvaig got to his feet and helped Nial and then the very tired Cailan out from under the great smooth stone. The fresh tingle of the dawn enfolded them, filling their nostrils with the heavy, dank scents of trees and undergrowth. High overhead, the paling sky showed in a leafy gap. In the dim light Nial could see quite well, and yet was considerably startled when a nearby boulder said: 'Ah! You very quickly! Peace to you!' and turned into Shetelig! He came over to them.

Ranvaig held up a hand. 'They could be follow, brother! They know our cave! We must go well, now. These boys is tired and Cailan is sore leg. We help him on each side.'

'Is only two, brother?'

Nial realised the question was about Finnian and Aengus. 'Yes,' he said, and tagged wearily along behind as the three monks started off through the trees. Presently he could see that Cailan was almost being carried. He was hopping from time to time, always on the one foot. It was only when the trees began to thin out that Nial saw how badly swollen the other ankle still was.

'Wouldn't he like a rest?' he puffed, catching up.

'I am all right.'

'Shame on you, Brother! You speak lying! But is no matter, we must be still going.' Nial could not remember which of the twins was which in the half light; even their voices sounded similar.

'Where are we heading for?' he asked.

One of them flung an arm out ahead. 'Small boat yust there.'

At that moment they cleared the edge of the wood and before them lay a silver expanse of water. At first Nial thought it was part of the Narrows through which the tide rushed to fill and empty the lough itself, and it was with quite a shock of re-orientation that he realised that it was in fact the deep indentation to the west of Strangford.

They halted and looked carefully to each side along the shore. To their immediate right was a low grassy hump projecting out into the water. On the left a tree-clad promontory stood sharply against the misty, lower land to the south. The sudden rippling call of a curlew came singing over the still air from somewhere under the dark shore opposite, otherwise all was silent, grey, and motionless. Lying on the mud, just clear of the stony beach, the dim shape of a small boat could indeed be seen. The twins stopped and made a chair for Cailan with their arms.

'Is many holes in this boat. If we are not quickly, it will not be useful,' said one of them, and they hurried off towards the water's edge. Nial started after them, but almost immediately paused and listened. Over the wooded hill behind them, a rising volume of shouting was heard. He bent low and sprinted down through the long grass, his already sore feet, further cut and bruised in that awful tunnel, now being pricked and scratched by tiny thistles. The gull-broken shells of the foreshore didn't help either, and just as he slipped and fell on the slimy seaweed, he saw Ranvaig and Shetelig go down as well, dropping Cailan with a mighty splash into the mud.

'Will clean you,' came a low voice. 'That hide-hole smelly! Ah! Look there! They come!'

Nial glanced back and saw dim figures running among the trees far to his left. Hauling the boat along with them—it was a curious, part-dug-out, part-planked affair—they hurriedly splashed on into the deepening water. At last they paused and hoisted Cailan over the dark side. He rolled inboard with a splash and a rush of water.

'The thing's half sinking,' cried Nial. 'It'll never support all of us!'

'Ach!' spluttered Cailan, spitting out a mouthful of sea, 'I will have it bailed in a moment, if I can find the scoop. Here it is, too!'

'Now!' puffed Ranvaig. 'All we push and swim!'

Holding on with one hand, Nial and the two monks pulled the boat through the cold greyness as fast as they could, but the drag of their garments was an awful disadvantage. Nial suggested stopping to get them off.

'No time!' called Cailan, fairly throwing the water out. 'They have seen us now, and are nearly at the shore. I will—have her—empty enough soon and you can—all get in and —row.'

It was very deep now, and they were swimming properly, but slowly. Between the splashes of the scoopfuls of water, not to mention his own breathless panting, Nial could hear the shouting behind them grow louder and less frequent as their pursuers reached and entered the sea. He had a horrible mental picture of the somewhat similar occasion back at Lang-ey, and the subsequent fighting on the longship. And with all his soul he wanted no repetition.

'In now!' yelled Cailan, and collapsed into the remaining inch or two of bilge water. Shetelig and Ranvaig, on opposite sides of the craft, hove themselves in simultaneously, and Nial clambered in over the pointed stern. There were three thwarts, but only two oars, and the burly twins did the rowing. With the first few strokes, however, one thing became rapidly clear; provided the extremely flexible oars did not break, they were going to get away with it. They were outpacing the dark splashing heads that bobbed in their wake with considerable ease.

Cailan sat up, gasping, and glanced astern, his face a pale blob in the half light. He turned and grinned at Nial. 'Much like past moments—but rather pleasanter this time.' He peered at the high, tree-covered land already looming close ahead. 'Even if the bottom falls from our craft, and it may very well do so, I think we could reach the shore with a fair advantage.'

And indeed the bottom did fall out, or rather in, for they grounded the aged vessel on a particularly sharp rock not three yards from the weed-covered boulders of the beach. Slipping and scrambling, they made their way rapidly up into the trees, stopping only briefly to help Cailan when he stumbled, and to take what they hoped would be a last glance at the swimmers still struggling after them in the silent waters of the inlet. Up at the head of it, on their left, they could see a sort of weaving procession working its way along at a steady pace, the movement reflecting faintly in the water.

'Is boggy there,' muttered Shetelig, eyeing the slow advance. 'But they will soon round here, and follow the path where they think we run. So we keep up on rough places. Is long walk to your boat, friend Nial, so we go now.' And he threw an arm round Cailan, helping him on and up into the tangled undergrowth. Together the four of them climbed steeply, crossed a well-worn path almost at right-angles and climbed on. Their clothing slapped wetly about them. Nial suddenly gasped. His mind must be running slow, or something.

'You did say *my* boat, didn't you?' he puffed.

'You not mind, we hope. We think it maybe faster to row than skin boat. But are not sure, now. Was different, so.'

'But where is she now?'

'In bay by some islands. We would have come nearer to save walks, but think your boat not safe perhaps in the strong current. Sorry.'

'Oh, don't apologise, please! I'm delighted! I'd much rather you had brought *Cuan* than any of the monastery boats.'

'Ouch! What is wrong with them?' Cailan was being very brave with the punishment his ankle was taking.

'Oh. Er, nothing that I know of. It's just that, well, there's some food stowed away in *Cuan*'s bow, and I wouldn't mind sharing it with you.'

'Ach, Nial! What a good thing you did not speak of that before! I should have lost my wits thinking about it!' And the puffing twins found their charge almost breaking away from them in a sudden burst of speed.

After a while Cailan panted, 'How, by the Saints—did you know where—to look for us in the first place?'

'We see everything, from the Bell House.'

'Yes,' gasped Nial, wishing he had more stamina, 'but how did you know they'd bring us *here*? They could have killed us on that island—I still can't think why they didn't.'

'Ah, by then we are working out what they are doing on Lang-ey. And we think, if they catch prisoners, maybe they would be make saying where the rest of the treasure is taken. Is what they think. We know when later we catch view of all walking along shore. Is certain then.'

For a while they all struggled on upwards without anyone speaking. Even the sounds of their pursuers had faded into the distance below them, and before very long they found themselves breaking out of the trees on to rougher, hummocky ground. Gradually the sun rose and began to warm their backs. The land fell away to the right, and they now skirted round the curve of the hill in a generally westerly direction.

Shetelig led between two great grey hunks of outcropping rock.

'Now, look,' he said. 'There is pathway, down there in the valley. Peoples is often there. Look! See a man runs there? And there? We must not be see! Danes will not wait to kill this times.'

Working now from one clump of gorse, bramble or rock to the next, they continued down more cautiously.

'About them finding the treasure gone,' said Ranvaig suddenly, 'is this true? They know how much misses?'

'Almost exactly.' Cailan's voice now sounded tight with pain. 'Fortunately for Nial and me, they did not work out who had been removing it until we were at the settlement. Why they did not kill us then, I know not. One of them tried to.'

There was a short silence. Nial saw the two Danes glance at each other and back at Cailan.

'They will raid Aendrum for this treasure. We know how they work their minds.'

'We know them too,' nodded Cailan. 'And you are right. Indeed, there is only one reason why they have not already set out.' And he outlined what they had heard in and under the longhouse, and how the warships were away, and about the young Lief Thorsson.

'Who is this?'

'Grandson of Eric Haroldsson, we think.'

'Haroldsson!' The two brothers gasped.

'Yes, he seemed to be acting as Chief until the other man comes back.'

'Cedric Fairhead.'

'We think so.'

'Haroldsson will stop for no one! He will be oldly now, though.'

'That's right,' said Nial. 'With a sort of claw hand.'

Ranvaig turned and grabbed him by the shoulder. 'By the Heavens! You did not see the man?'

'We did, up in the longhouse. Actually he was rather nice to us, on the whole. Stopped this little red-head from killing us outright.'

'Why?'

The unexpected question brought him up all standing. 'Why? Well—er, Cailan reckons it was because he was so disgusted with Lief Whatsit for losing one of the precious longships to a handful of monks.'

'Is more than that,' broke in Shetelig. 'But come, we must cross that pathway soon. Is long way round, but those who follows go faster than we. Quickly on, now. No, is right. This Eric Haroldsson would want more than plain murder for you. He has good reason for not liking monks too many. Is his three fingers is cut off by our Abbot Tholrykr in young days—after burying that treasure. So we hear as children story. I bless the angels that my brother is guessing right where they are hiding you.'

'How *did* you know, Ranvaig?' asked Nial. 'The exact place, I mean.'

'Ah! I did not, really. I yust thinks. And I thinks that anyway, if you are not under the longhouse, and nobody else is, then door of it is not going to be hard shut, and I am already so far into the village without they see me. But here you were! Is good. What is worry now, is can we get our words to good Abbot Sedna, before the sons of our uncles get their swords to him?'

The cold thought curdled in Nial's mind, and they hurried on down the hill. What with the general scrub, clumps of gorse, and one thing and another, they did not see the line of men approaching at speed along the pathway until they were practically on top of them. Flinging themselves behind a bramble thicket, they lay with thumping hearts as the group raced by. Nial had a young gorse-bush flattened and very prickly under him, its juicy spikes biting through his thin linen tunic with every heaving breath he took.

They were not seen.

As the last warrior passed out of sight down the lane, both Shetelig and Ranvaig said 'Amen,' and stood up with such precision of timing that they might have been drilled to it.

The rest of the journey across the floor of the valley and up over the ridge towards the southern shore of the lough took a very long time. Cailan was quite plainly incapable of hurrying, however much he wanted to. At first Nial was terrified that their desperately slow daylight progress would be spotted, but then quite suddenly they noticed distant objects were starting to grow faint and disappear. Bringing the sharp tang of salt with it, a dense fog rolled slowly in from the sea.

'God be praised!' puffed Cailan, hobbling towards it with all his remaining energy.

He didn't go far. Nial, staggering along behind him, his own feet leaving smears of blood on the ground, saw him fall. With never a word, Ranvaig and Shetelig again made a chair with their hands and even took turns carrying the utterly exhausted Cailan on their backs, for he was almost unconscious, and his ankle looked hideously bloated.

How often they strayed from the shortest route to the lough shore, Nial could only guess. Several times they realised they were heading the wrong way, but it was difficult not to. Then at last, an uncertain brightness high to their right resolved itself into the pale, hazy outline of the sun. Carefully manoeuvring to keep it just behind their right shoulders, the Danish twins plodded on with their burden, and Nial forced himself to keep close. There were times when the fog lay thicker in the bowl of a hollow, or where the ground grew marshy at the source of a streamlet, and it would then become impossible to tell even approximately which way the ball of the sun lay. Once, they crested a small hillock to find a thinning of the fog and the yellow sphere high in the sky ahead of them!

They passed grazing deer that stared loftily after them, antlered heads held motionless and high. There was the blood-tingling moment when they were suddenly confronted with the dim outline of a man, and flung themselves down among the long, soaking grass; but he went on his way without seeing them.

At last they reached the top of a steep, grassy cliff, and sliding and slithering amongst the briars and thorn trees, scrambled down. Nial's already torn tunic caught on a branch and half the side of it ripped open before he could stop himself. Only the woven belt held it together now.

They reached level ground some forty feet below, and stood among stones and grass, peering about them. A thick dark line of wave-swept seaweed together with a grey border of rounded stones and some reddish clay, marked the shoreline, but the tide had still some four and a half hours to come, and was out of sight in the fog. They could hear it, restlessly washing the beach with its little wavelets. On either side of them the land curved round, so that they knew they were in a small bay. There was nothing else in sight.

'Which way to the boat?' asked Cailan weakly. Nial was longing to see *Cuan* again, and could barely resist dashing off to search for her.

'By there,' Ranvaig pointed to the right. 'A smaller bay than this.'

They tottered over the uneven ground, greyness and large round boulders everywhere about them; and following the line of rotting sea-wrack, they practically fell into *Cuan* before they noticed her. Everything was there, the mast standing proudly upwards into the mist, the oars (not too neatly stowed), sail, spars, motor, the lot, dripping with moisture, but real and *there*. Nial was almost jumping with delight, but his feet were too sore.

'Now,' sighed Ranvaig, plumping himself down on the stones, 'all we have to be doing is waiting.'

'Waiting?' Nial thought again of the utter urgency of the whole operation, of all the long waits and delays he had already endured, when every second could be of vital importance to the lives of those at Aendrum.

'Yes, waiting. And having faith.'

'But why? What for?'

'For that the Danes cannot go Veeking in fog. Nor can we risk losing *us* in the lough, either! The fog is for us to have rest in, safely. Rest, and praying.' And at that the three monks knelt, side by side with bowed heads, on the stones of the beach. Nial looked at them and thought that he would leave it to the experts. His whole mind was dazed, too weak to argue; fatigued with the entire kaleidoscope of events. And hunger. Hunger! The food in *Cuan*'s locker!

Leaning over the dew-damp gunwale he reached down and opened the locker door. Some ropes fell out, but he slung them back and pulled at the duffle-bag. It was green with mildew. He tugged at its soggy strings and peered in. To his deep dismay, the package that had been a loaf of fresh white bread was covered in a puff of green growth, and he threw it out in a spasm of disgust. Perhaps the change of time had made everything rot, he thought, and then he saw the two oranges remaining from his lunch, so long ago it seemed, on Wood Island. They were fine and healthy-looking! Half of one each! *And* the chocolate, too! Two whole bars of it! Then he found the tin of beans, the can-opener, the pan, the polythene-wrapped box of matches, and the stove. He set that up on the floorboards there and then, turned on the gas-tap and struck a match.

The 'plop' and roar of the lighting stove brought the heads of the three monks up like Jack-in-the-boxes. They saw Nial stooping over the ring of blue flame in the boat, and grabbed at each other. Then slowly, Cailan relaxed a bit.

'What magic now is this, Mo-Nial?' His voice quavered uncertainly. 'Whatever are you creating?'

Despite himself, Nial smiled. 'I want to heat these beans; that's all.'

'Ach! How you joke! What beans? I do not think I like jokes about food!—What are those yellow balls?'

Nial knew he could surprise them by opening the can of beans, but it had not occurred to him that none of them had ever seen or tasted, let alone even heard of oranges!

It was a good, and for Nial a very amusing meal. His three guests were bewildered. First there were the strange reddish beans that came out of the little cylinder of what looked like shiny iron, instead of off a plant; then there was the delicious taste of them when they had been warmed on the apparently fuel-less fire that burned with such noise and ferocity. Later came the weird and sweet brown stuff that Nial unwrapped from, of all things, an incredibly thin sheet of silver! But their curiosity reached almost fever-pitch when he began to peel away the thick skin of the golden oranges to reveal the oddest and certainly the juiciest fruit they had ever come across.

They couldn't get over the way it had grown in tightly packed little sections within itself, and they spent much time comparing one piece with another. All too soon, everything was finished. But little though each helping had been, Nial began to feel better, and to think clearer, too. It was now almost ten o'clock—almost the middle of the tide. It was queer how the tidal cycle had remained unbroken when he changed periods. But now, he realised, if it hadn't got in the evening before, the longship fleet could come up the Narrows from the sea as soon as the fog lifted! Why he had allowed himself to be talked into this further wait, he could not imagine! He had a chart, after all! Rousing the others, he said so.

'But the fog, Nial—' Cailan protested vehemently. 'No one goes afloat in fog!'

'Why not, for goodness sake? We can steer by the sun, same as we did on land! Oh, come on! We have so little time to warn the Abbot. What's the good of waiting until the Danes set out too? Come *on*!'

'Are you *sure* you can steer us straight?' Cailan hopped along beside them as they launched *Cuan* over the weed and down the glutinous mud to the water.

'Should be possible while I can see the sun astern of us, but someone will have to keep a good look-out forward. Here, give me a hand with the oars, this one's jammed under the thwart.'

'I put it there, I get it out,' said Ranvaig. They scrambled in, and helping Cailan into the stern, Nial found the twins again taking over the rowing. He did not object, for all the mighty splashes; he genuinely doubted if he himself could row very far. The many and severe bruises he had collected in the last couple of days were now making movement of any kind hurt more than a little. But there was no time to be idle, for all that. He found and studied the chart.

'Had you not better use that steering thing?' Cailan whispered. 'I do not think my Brothers are taking us very straight.'

It was true. The water was still extremely shallow, and many weedheads slipped by. Nial could see for himself that their course was snaking a good deal. He shipped the rudder, and peered ahead into the grey blanket that hung low on the smooth water. Somewhere close were a couple of islands, but after them it would be clear for quite a distance, out into the middle of the lough. *That* was going to be tricky.

The water deepened, and Nial, hand on tiller, kept *Cuan* as nearly with the hazy sun glistening in her wake as he could. At last he felt quite sure the islands were well astern, even though they had never once showed up, and now he steered rather more to port. He glanced at the chart again. There was open water as far as the Long Rock and Dunnyneill Island. If he could just find them, or even get clear past them to the long coast of Island Taggart, the rest would be almost easy. Thereafter it would only be a question of skirting the shore most of the time, and they would go right up through Ringhaddy Sound, and past Darragh, Trasnagh and Rainey. Why, they'd be at Aendrum in no time!

He looked over his shoulder again at the sun. Hmm . . . A bit too far to one side. It was now well past ten, if his watch was still right, so the sun should be to the east of south. What an idiot he was not to have brought a compass! Get the sun-path in the sea a bit more over the wake. There! That should be about right—Oh! And suddenly he found himself staring at a large piece of land, one of the two islands they had just passed between! The other one was appearing also! Then to his dismay, the sheltering mist seemed to pull back and away, as though drawn aside by a giant hand, and the very shore of the lough itself loomed out of it! He could see trees and the cliff they had come down.

Ranvaig and Shetelig, facing aft on the rowing thwart, watched the land being exposed with widening eyes, and without a word began to pull harder on the oars. Their increased jerking as *Cuan* spurted through the oily water made Cailan turn to see what they had seen, and in doing so it was he who first spotted the leading longship pulling clear of the Narrows, far to the right.

'Nial!'

Nial saw not only the first longship, but the curved prow of the second also appearing from behind the point of land. With a sinking heart, he knew then that the fleet had come home.

'We are doomed!' Cailan turned, despairing in his weakness and pain. 'We will never get to Aendrum before them! They can row at great speed, those Danes.'

But Nial wasn't giving up so easily. Not now. '*We* have Danes at the oars, too, Cailan!' he cried, 'and I'll have the "outboard" going in a minute, if you'll just lift your feet while I get it out. Mind!'

'Ouch!' The metal propeller rapped the swollen ankle, and shocked Cailan into a more hopeful frame of mind. 'Can I help at all?'

'Yes, here! Take the rudder from me.' With as much haste as Nial could safely muster, he lowered the heavy little motor over the transom and began screwing up its clamps.

'They turn back! See? They turn back!' Ranvaig had stopped rowing and was pointing excitedly. There was no doubt about it. The foremost longship was indeed swinging round, away from them!

'The fog!' cried Cailan. 'It is because the fog has gone! I do believe they thought to creep up to Aendrum unseen, just like ourselves! Now that the fog has gone they will wait for nightfall. I feel sure of it. Look! The second boat is turning, too!'

The long profile of the second craft altered. She seemed to shorten and they saw the row of war-shields shine and the sunlight glint as the great bank of oars rose and fell—then paused. She turned no further. And suddenly the oars churned into the water once more, lifted, and bit their waves again, and Nial knew that this time it was *Cuan* that was their target! Feverishly he switched on the petrol and flooded the carburettor. A twist of the throttle lever, and a violent tug on the starting cord, and the motor burst into life. *Cuan* surged forward, and there was a moment of flurried excitement as Shetelig found his oar digging into the rushing water. He was not used to the broad, curved blades, less to the speed engendered by a propeller, and the boat heeled frantically to the pressure before he turned the oar right way and yanked it dripping from the water.

At full throttle the engine drove them over the calm still sea, the bow-wave foaming and tumbling and hissing past to the wake astern.

It was impossible to tell so soon just whether or not they were gaining anything on the longship. What was clear was that the other one had completed a circle and was also rowing in hot pursuit. Nial could plainly see the sheets of spray leap from under her forefoot with every thrust of the gleaming oars. Ahead he could at last faintly discern the outline of an island. It—it *should* have been Dunnyneill—but instead of being one high island with a low spit or tail running out eastwards (it was often called Rat Island because of this configuration), it was two distinct and almost equally high mounds. Only the thin line of the Long Rock off its west side convinced him that it was the same place and that he was seeing it before someone had removed soil and stone from one half to build up and perhaps fortify the other. He hoped he was right, and swung *Cuan* round so as to head close to the east of it. And then the motor faltered, and under his agonised gaze, died. He sprang round to deal with it, hastily winding the starting-cord round its groove on the flywheel. He pulled, but nothing happened. It just wouldn't fire! A glimpse of the longships as he wound the rope again showed them looking appreciably closer.

'Row!' he yelled. 'Row for all you can!' And he heard the oars clatter into place and felt the boat lift forwards. What on earth could be wrong with the thing? And then it dawned on him, and he hastily unscrewed the tiny plug in the filler cap that let air into the tank to replace the used petrol. In forgetting to open it he had created a partial vacuum, and the fuel had stopped running. In a twinkling the motor was buzzing strongly again, and this time Shetelig got his oar clear in good time.

Dunnyneill drew slowly nearer—it really did seem to be it. They were now at any rate holding the Danes. How long the the petrol would last out was a matter of luck. Nial wished he hadn't used so much of it on the 'Fire Iron' demonstration. What was it his father had said? Only use it when necessary? Well, it was certainly that at this moment! Ranvaig and Shetelig were thrilled with it, of course. They did not know that it would splutter to a halt before long, and for good. Fortunately, neither did their ex-compatriots in the ships astern, or they wouldn't be trying so hard to catch up now. The job would be easier later. And at that Nial realised he was looking back at not two, but four longships! Even as he watched, a fifth swept into view from the Narrows. The sun flashed on something high on her bow— and as she swung into the wake of her sisters, he saw the golden dragon's head on her proud stempost show clear against the opposite shore. She was rapidly overhauling the rest of the fleet.

There could be no doubting now that their ultimate destination must be Aendrum.

'Is there not anything we can be doing?' Ranvaig and his twin had also seen the new arrival, and were plainly worried. 'That is Chief Veeking boat. Is Cedric Fairhead himself!'

'Yes.' Nial had guessed as much. 'You—and Cailan, sit as still as you can, but pray as hard as you are able. And keep praying.'

And presently the wind came through.

First it merely darkened the water in the distance, away over to starboard. But gradually, the line of ripples spread nearer.

'Cailan! Hold the motor for me! We must get the sail on her!'

Cailan stared at Nial in disbelief—then at the vibrating engine. His mouth fell open. Nial grabbed the thin hand that waved uncertainly in mid-air and planted it firmly on the jiggling, rubber-covered tiller.

'Go on, man! It works just like the other thing, and you managed that perfectly the other day.' And he began to scramble forward between the other two to get at the halyard and loose the sail. *Cuan* commenced to swing wildly to starboard. The turn tightened.

'The other way! Push it the other way!' Nial clung on as the boat rocked violently to the reversed helm, and with the wake snaking and curving, *Cuan* continued erratically in the direction of Dunnyneill. Nial had the sail up and fluttering to the air created by their own forward speed just before the real wind came through to them. Jamming the iron centre-plate down in its slot, he scrambled aft and snatched in the flicking end of the mainsheet, pinning the sail in flat. *Cuan* heeled to the pressure of it and the whine of the motor rose with the increasing speed. Cailan looked terrified, and was relieved beyond measure when Nial took over from him.

'You pray well,' said Nial, glancing astern. 'Look how the wind has come! And well forward of the beam at that! Your Viking men can't use their sails in this. *They* must row still! Pray some more, and maybe it will last!' And the three heads bowed again. He prayed a bit himself, though without taking his eyes from the islands ahead, and the trim of the straining sail. It was an old sail, made of cotton cloth, not one of the modern synthetics, and he feared that the strain put upon it by this rushing motor-sailing would be too much for it. It had mildewed badly after that downpour at the start of all this, and he could only hope that this had not sapped any more of its failing strength. The breeze was grand though, and in just the very best direction possible. Maybe things were going in their favour at last!

Dunnyneill seemed to be almost rushing towards them now, and in minutes it was close abeam. For all its peculiar shape, Nial barely spared it a look, for to his delight the wind had started to veer round a little, and still keeping the sail full, he could head more directly north. Indeed, he managed by pinching up a fraction just once or twice, to steer actually to the east of the group of drying shoals marked on his chart just beyond the island. It was a very shallow place, and the risk of suddenly wrapping a weed-head round the propeller was considerable, but he held on, squeezing the throttle wide open all the time, and juggling with an inch or two of sheet in order continually to get the most out of the taut sail.

As the wind freshened, he got Cailan to join him on the weather side, to try and keep the boat as upright as possible. The unstayed mast was bending ominously, and he tried hard not to look at it. Spray hissed and rattled across, stinging and soaking them.

For fully a mile more there was comparatively clear water,

and then at last they would come abreast of the long string of islands that curved round with the western side of the lough. He would have to decide whether to go inside them and risk losing the wind, or pass outside some at least, and risk being slowed by waves if the breeze increased further. If the engine stopped before they reached Mahee, and he felt sure that it must, the further they were to windward, the better. The passage through the sound inside the biggest of the islands would be almost certainly dead to windward for a good deal of the way, and the sail would be of little use. He must go outside. Again he glanced at the following ships. The gap, without a shadow of doubt, had in fact widened. He held her as close up to the wind as he dared.

They were abreast of the eastern end of the first of the chain of islands when the engine ran out of petrol. But before Nial had time to bother about the Vikings, he was suddenly fully occupied in coping with a runaway *Cuan*. Up to that minute, the normal steering of the outboard had given him full directional control. It had not crossed his mind that when the motor stopped, so would this effect. The boat, now rudderless, swung up into the wind and flipped about on the other tack, catching all of the crew unawares and on the wrong side. There was a frantic scramble as she heeled over and water came spewing in, but Nial let fly the sheet and she righted.

'Bail!' he shouted. And then with the momentary panic subsiding, he added more quietly, 'There's a bucket under the foredeck.'

With the sail flogging above him and *Cuan* making odd little forward swoops as she backed and filled, Nial wasted no time in getting the useless motor off its bracket and back inboard. But in his rush to ship the rudder he fumbled with the business of properly locating its hangings, and he had to make two attempts, leaning over the transom. Every time he tried to get the bottom pintle down into its gudgeon, the sail seemed to fill deliberately, creating a sideways pressure on the deep rudder-blade which forced it out of alignment just as he was getting it in. At last it dropped home, and he turned, grabbed the tiller, sheeted in the sail, and as soon as *Cuan* had picked up enough speed to carry her through the wind's eye, he banged the helm across and spun her round. This time the others were quicker at getting their weight over to balance her as she heeled on the original tack, and Nial noticed Cailan looking surprisingly smug with himself. He, after all, had sailed to windward in the boat before, which was more than his Brother monks had done, and he had foreseen the necessity of the manoeuvre and explained to them what would happen. But what concerned Nial was the reduced speed at which they were now travelling, for without the thrust of the engine which had resulted in an apparently high windspeed, the present breeze could barely be described as 'fresh'. For all that, *Cuan* was still splashing along at a most reasonable pace, and though he thought about it, it was most unlikely that the oars would help. The thing was, could he squeeze her sufficiently up to windward to clear Dunsy Rock, the tiny off-lying islet which now lay in their course away ahead? At low tide it was joined by a drying reef all the way across to the big island on his left. He turned to squint aft at the longships, and was horrified to find them already closer than the last time he had looked; Cedric Fairhead was in the lead. He stared back at the chart.

'Why did the Fire Iron stop?' Cailan's tone was practically conversational.

'No more "petrol"! But do be quiet, *please*! I've got to think!' Nial didn't even look up. Now he was feeling the heavy responsibility known to any sea captain whose ship and crew are in danger or difficulty. It was up to him, and him alone, somehow to outwit the enemy and sail his boat to safety. He wondered if, supposing he suddenly made a detour, say off to the other side of the lough even, would the Danes follow? Or would they just head straight on up to attack the monastery, without his then being in a position to warn them at all? And if they did follow, what then? No! He must go on straight for Mahee, and somehow, somewhere, lose them on the way. He brushed the windswept hair out of his face and peered ahead with screwed up eyes. *Cuan* would only just pass east of Dunsy Rock on this tack. The Danes were rowing still, and rowing fast, and he knew he couldn't really afford to turn at right-angles to their path even for a very brief tack.

In a flash of inspiration it came to him!

'Cailan! Or better still, Ranvaig! How well do the Danes know this part of the lough?'

'Oh, they mostly pass outside of here because the shallowings makes much winding. Or inside this big island there, up the sound.'

'The—the "shallowings"—do they know them well?'

'Oh, they touch them sometimes, and afterwards keep away. They have no picture, there, like yours! Is wonderful!'

'Good,' said Nial, and with brightened eyes he headed straight for the broad and utterly innocent-looking gap to the *west* of Dunsy Rock. His watch told him there was still just under three hours of tide to go, but he knew that *Cuan* could skate clear over the barely covered reef. He hoped the longships would be just too deep.

They were catching up terribly quickly. Even as he approached the unseen shoal, Nial realised that the Danes would still overtake him if they did happen to know of the reef and made a detour round the other side of Dunsy Rock. It was close on the port bow, now. In a moment he would need the centre-plate up, or mostly so anyway. Still the water looked deep. *Cuan* slipped on, her crew silent. Even Shetelig and Ranvaig had not realised what he was doing. Down in the water he suddenly saw the dark weed wavering in the slow current.

'Lift the plate!'

Shetelig stared at him in complete puzzlement.

'That thing! The iron thing there! Yes, that! Up with it, as quick as you can!'

Cuan seemed to hesitate as the brown weed clutched at the toe of the centre-board, but Shetelig was already lifting it.

'That'll do! Can you hold it like that? Don't bring it up any more till I tell you. And whatever you do, don't drop it!'

He could see the stones now, racing slyly by beneath them, rising nearer and nearer. *Cuan* was side-slipping a good deal with the plate presenting such a reduced area to the water, but it would have to come up even further.

'More! More up!'

It was right up now, for Shetelig, not in the least understanding the purpose of the heavy object, had practically lifted it right out of its case. They were crabbing sideways, and the rudder was pulling viciously. For a ghastly second Nial felt the tiller jerk and tremble under his hand, but the sea-bed fell away as suddenly as it had risen, and they were free.

'Plate down again, please, Shetelig. And thank you.'

With the boat properly balanced once more, Nial resettled himself to the task of getting the utmost speed out of her, luffing her up a little only to have a clear course past what his chart called 'Gull Rock', and then heading just to the windward side of the higher and much larger island ahead, where the breeze would not be hindered. He had no need to watch the longships.

If they knew of the reef, they would clear it. If they did not, they couldn't miss it.

Cailan gasped, his mouth falling open in astonishment, and Nial knew. With a surge of relief in his heart, all his hopes were fulfilled! He joyfully turned to gaze astern to see that the leading ship had run full tilt up the reef and careered over on her side, the gilded dragon-head high and at a crazy angle, and her oars waving in spiky confusion. The second boat had only just been overtaken by her, and struck practically at the same moment. Her mast snapped and disappeared over the row of shields into the water. Of the three craft astern, one was curving wildly round across the bows of the next, but in seconds was shuddering to a halt herself even while the other, in a riot of shouting, back-paddled furiously and received a vicious dunt in the stern and a succession of splintered oars as the fifth and final boat lost control and careered into her. Everywhere men were leaping into the water to push and heave at the curving sides of their great vessels.

It would take them quite a time to get sorted out. The pity of it was that the ships were so strongly built, and the shoal was only large stones and not sharp rocks which might have made a more permanent job of them.

Aboard *Cuan*, Cailan was beside himself with exuberance, and the Danish twins were literally bouncing, so that Nial had to beseech them to be still, for fear they would capsize the boat or break something! They regarded him with renewed and almost solemn respect, and then sat as peacefully as they could, hugging each other close and grinning all over their great swarthy faces.

And so it was, that when *Cuan* eventually arrived at the stony shores of Aendrum, she had a considerable lead over the 'Veekings'.

10

Fire and Sword

A long line of the brown-robed monks waited for them on the foreshore, so there were plenty of people to hear. All around them, expressions changed from happy greeting to deep concern as Nial and Cailan shouted their warnings of the imminent raid, even before they were out of the boat. Someone saw Cailan hobble and wince as he came ashore, and he was hoisted shoulder high and rushed up the hill and past the guarded gateways in the cashel walls to the foot of the Bell House. The Saint's bell was already beginning to jangle urgently from the pointed cap of the tower.

Nial almost got left behind, for he was aching from head to foot, and felt terribly stiff after being so long at the helm. Friendly arms helped him up the steeply sloping ground, and gasps of astonishment rose round him as Ranvaig told what had happened, how they had been captured, and why. Nial half listened, all the zest gone from him. The goal had been achieved. Aendrum was warned. He wanted so badly to rest, to relax—but even as he staggered on under the weight of exhaustion, he realised with a pang of desperation that his troubles were hardly begun! Troubles! This place he had stretched every nerve and muscle to reach, as if it were home, a place he knew, was on the very brink of battle, the outcome of which he could only guess. What would happen to him, he had no idea. How did dreams end, anyway? It had to be a dream, now. He couldn't bear it to be otherwise. And yet—everywhere about him people were running, this way and that. With much shouting and arm-waving, various herds of animals were being shooed into different enclosures. As he entered the second cashel he could see long staves of wood being handed out to a rapidly forming group, and great clouds of steam were issuing from the foundry huts on his left and from the distant Cooking House too, where the fires were also being put out. Only one flame would be left burning in a carefully guarded lamp, so that things could be got going again afterwards. Afterwards? Nial wondered if there would be an afterwards.

'The Abbot wants you.'

Oh, lord! He felt so weary, he didn't see how he could possibly climb the great ladder up into the Bell House. But he didn't have to.

Prime Abbot Sedna O'Deman had already come down from his room to greet Cailan, and was now standing listening as the battered young monk gave him the gist of their story. When he saw Nial, he turned and hastened towards him, looking suddenly older, and yet worried and welcoming at the same time.

'Nial of Ross!' The slow, deeply intoned words had just the edge of urgency in them. 'I have to thank you again for the life of my beloved Cailan; and even more for your skill in safely bringing us the awful warning of assault! We have long known the Danes would attack us if they found we had taken their treasure. The Great Father has watched with you, my son, and so may He watch with us all, now! It is His blessing on us that you are here, for with you among us we may not all perish.'

Nial stared at the small white figure, and was not at all sure.

'Fear nothing, my son! *You* shall not be hurt! Can you fight, my boy? Och, me! Of course you can! Cailan has said much about that, and far less of the danger we now face. But you are bruised! Indeed you are! I will send someone for the Herb

Grower. She will give you something to help the pain, and to strengthen you, too.'

'Thank you,' said Nial. The wrinkled face turned full towards him, and he felt a thin and gentle hand on his arm.

'My son. It is for us to thank you! Not just for what you have already accomplished in bringing us warning, but for what you will yet have to do. My blood is Celtic, my son, just as yours is. I know in my bones too that the fulfilment of your task and Purpose is very near. Now, there is much I must see to. Aendrum has not suffered the fury of a Veeking raid in many generations. I fear we are not as ready as we might be. God be with you, my son.' And with that he moved smoothly away to join a group of monks standing under the brilliant decoration of the church's west gable.

Nial saw the old Abbot several times in the next half hour or so; the little man somehow seemed to be almost everywhere he looked, the bald head nodding and the wrinkled face smiling quiet confidence to all and sundry. Only one other person was smiling, and that was because she always did. Bronach was already up in the Cooking House soaking bunches of various leaves from her herb garden in the last of the hot water, and it was not long before she came scurrying round to find Nial and give him a hornful of a warm, greenish infusion that tasted strongly of something very like lemons. She grinned at him while he forced himself to drink all but the very last dregs of it, shaking her head from side to side, and muttering that she never thought she'd get 'healing the likes of him'. When he had dutifully swallowed what he could she offered him a sip from the clay pot she was cuddling in the crook of her arm. Nial handed back his horn, but peering into the steaming liquid, shook his head.

'What is it?'

'Courage! What else would I be handin' out afore a fight?' Her voice crackled high above the general bustle and excitement that filled the air. 'I've the other things for healin' wounds ready for later.' She paused. 'Good luck to ye, son! And tell them about old hole-in-the-head Bronach when ye get home!' And she lurched away on her lanky legs, her brown hair blowing to one side and clearly showing off the round scar. Get home, he thought. Oh, if only he could!

Already the island folk were beginning to file in along the causeway and up through the ancient twisting entrances past the well. The women, many carrying babies and young children, hurried right on up into the inner cashel itself, while their menfolk spread themselves out round the top of the outer wall. The weapons they held ranged widely indeed. Nial saw at least one stone axe, not to mention a number of bronze and a couple of highly prized iron versions with great curved cutting edges. One or two little round shields were held by some of the younger men, but almost everyone else had taken off their cloaks and wound or part-wound them round their left forearms. This left quite a number of them naked, but it was only when he saw some of them deliberately remove their clothes that he realised they were preparing for hand-to-hand fighting, when loose garments might be grabbed all too easily by one's opponent. Skin was more slippery!

He wished he had a cloak for a shield, and wondered what else he could use. If anyone pulled at his tunic, or what was left of it, it would fall away in their hands. He couldn't at that moment see the fleet of longships which were making their approach from behind Rainey Island, but he knew they, or at least some of them, couldn't be far away. If only he had a spear, or something! And then he saw Cailan hobbling towards him, and rushed over.

'Ach! Nial!' came the greeting. 'I wondered where you were! We have not been so separated in many hours! Bronach has rubbed my ankle with some of her plants, and bound these leaves on it. Very clever, too. Much of the pain is gone, and it is a better shape as well. She has wonderful hands, that one!'

'Cailan! What can I do to help?'

'Help, Mo-Nial? Nothing! Unless you know of some future magic that does even better than Bronach's brews.'

'No! I mean about the fight! What can I do, or where should I stand?'

'Stand? Ach now, I think it will be run, not stand.'

'I am *not* a coward!' Nial felt stung with indignation, but Cailan shook his head.

'I was not saying you were, for I know otherwise. But I have much doubt if we can hold the Danes back. They are skilled warriors; we are men of peace.' He spoke calmly, almost callously.

'But what about the islanders? They seem to have plenty of weapons! Quite a few of them seem to have perfectly good swords, apart from all the clubs and things. Oh, don't lose faith, Cailan! Not now! I'm sure we'll survive!'

'You, Mo-Nial, will. We are all praying for that. And those that run will, too, some of them. What was it you said? God helps those that help themselves? I think that is true, today.'

'I'm going to stay by you, Cailan, just as you've stayed with me these last few days. You once told me you only fought Danes. Well, just now I think that's a pretty good idea, so I'll join you. And it's no use saying ... Cailan!' He turned, grabbing Cailan's arm. 'I've just remembered! My boat! Oh, Cailan! Do they *have* to get my boat?'

It didn't take the young monk a second to see that at the back of his mind Nial was still connecting that strange craft with his passage home through time.

'Of course not!' he cried. 'Come though, we have not much time, I think. We can take it to the back of the island!' And as fast as his leaf-covered ankle would let him, he led Nial back down over the crowded, sunlit grass, towards the bay.

At each cashel they were held up. At the first and second gateways there were people carrying stones with which to narrow the gaps in the walls, and they had to push their way past and clamber over the part-built obstacles. The third gateway was already totally blocked and they had to climb up and jump from the full height of the great cashel. Somehow Cailan broke his fall on his good foot, and managed to stumble on.

They dragged *Cuan* into the water and tumbled over the side as she floated, water spraying from Cailan's leafy bandage. At once the current caught the boat and began to sweep them round. The wind had backed into the west but there was no time to set sail anyway. Each took an oar and dropped it into its rowlock. The first longship seemed almost to leap into view round the point of Rainey, skirting close along the shore inside the little islet there. *Cuan* spun as her oars bit into the swirling water of the narrows. 'Right!' yelled Nial, and they headed her full into the tideway, throwing all their weight and the strength of their thighs and backs into each stroke, so that the bow-wave hissed, and hissed again.

Once clear of the narrows they swung north-west, hugging the Mahee shore as close as they dared. It was only when abreast of the stone 'ablution quays' that they saw the ship of Cedric Fairhead himself bursting the tide round the other side of Rainey and passing cleanly between the spits of rock running out from it and the nearby mainland, the golden dragon flashing its fearsome face from the towering, arrogant stem-post.

For a moment Nial thought the longship was trying to cut them off, and he almost overcame the thrust of Cailan's pull in his efforts to increase speed even more.

'Ach!—I am—just not—able—to row—harder!'

'Sorry!' Nial missed a stroke and *Cuan* swung away from the shore again. They watched the long line of oars on the Danish ship pause as she too altered course—to make her final run-in to the shores of Aendrum. They watched the bobbing row of heads surging along behind the bank of the cashel wall, up on their right, gathering with up-raised spears nearest to this new line of attack. They saw the pointing arm in one of the top windows of the Bell House. Like the deathly hush before a violent storm; or the sudden, sinister silence that comes over a small boat in an ocean gale the instant before a giant wave strikes, all Aendrum was engulfed in a trembling stillness.

A rising roar of deep voices echoed from round in the bay, and Nial glanced at Cailan. The oval face was white like marble, the pale blue eyes raised in mute but fervent prayer. There was no fear in them; only tears. The Danes had landed, landed on his beloved Aendrum. Even now came the scream of a wounded man.

They rowed on.

The sweeping bow of Cedric Fairhead's ship ran high up the bouldered beach astern of them, but was hidden at once behind the splashes of sword- and axe-laden, helmeted warriors who leapt into the shallows, unshipping the gleaming, colourful row of shields as they went. It was with a kind of helpless fascination that Nial witnessed the massed charge up the steep slope as far as the grey and green line of the outer cashel. He could see how the effect of the rising ground, coupled with the weight of their chain-mail shirts and iron weapons, slowed the attackers appreciably as they neared the barrier. He could see how some of them pressed on their knees to gain extra climbing power, so that their swords waved and glinted in the sun. He watched a hail of stones flung from leather slings on the cashel-top, and saw the round shields lift to ward them off. He saw a spear flash up and fly vibrating in a clean curve, that ended suddenly in a Danish chest. The man slumped to the ground backwards so that the shaft stuck slanting into the air. And somehow the sight gave Nial a surge of super-strength, and he found that Cailan responded with him.

The shouting, and now the strange clattering noise of the attack reached his ears and then began to fade as they swung further round the island. The great outer wall itself disappeared from their sight behind the curve of trees that grew on the rounded side of the drumlin.

They left *Cuan* at the place where Nial had first run her aground in the cloudburst four days previously. Cailan showed surprise and gladness at this, for he had fully expected Nial to land on the next island instead. It was with deep friendship that he took Nial's helping hand as they scrambled up among the thorn-trees and brambles of Mahee, taking the way, the most direct way, up to the monastery.

As they climbed the steep hillside the noise grew rapidly louder again until with a clear view of the higher buildings, the full cacophony of mad, clashing, screaming sound burst upon them. Even as they rushed towards it on their tired and painful legs, a new strength seemed almost to lift and help them towards the stricken Abbey. Already the battle was well under way; groups of the helmeted Vikings were working their way round, trying to find an entrance in the massive walls that encircled their goal. Over the top of the cashel the defenders could be seen spreading out, too. Nial and the limping Cailan headed more to the east, where the low walls of the outer enclosure came nearest to the cashel. It was here that Bronach's herb plot lay, and here that the gate furthest from the main attack would be. It was easy enough getting over beside the herbs without being seen by the Danes, though already some of them had found their way on to the main part of the island, away to the left, and could be seen attempting to make an approach along the great causeway below. Naturally the cashel gateway at the garden was in part blocked, so that the two had to squeeze through, having first made sure that they were recognised by the guard and his armed band of nervous farmers.

'Come on,' shouted Cailan, 'we must get weapons!' and he hopped off towards the nearby eastern entrance of the middle cashel.

As they rounded a dividing wall in the terraced part of the area, they saw a small group of Vikings appear over a thinly guarded section of the outer defence, overcome a couple of boys hardly Nial's age, and jump down on to the grass of a fenced enclosure. The cows were at the far end of this—and so was one of the lads' friends, armed with a staff. He jabbed it at the nearest cow, fiercely, and let such a yelp out of him that the beast tore off in fright, gathering her fellow creatures about her as she galloped. The ensuing wild stampede ended in a bellowing panic of heaving cattle in a corner by the cashel, and four Danes, who lay still and crumpled in the grass behind them. Another was sitting up, hugging a very strangely angled arm and screaming.

Further to the south, yet another rush was driven back by a volley of hunting spears which their owners each flung with searing velocity from some kind of throwing-stick. That too cut down the effective number of the attackers. But they came again. Nial watched in a kind of daze as only a short way from him he saw the point of a returned spear appear out of the back of a man's head, and in a sort of stupefied slow-motion, he turned to see what caused a particularly piercing shriek on his right.

Some of the things Nial saw that afternoon were enough to turn the strongest stomach. His school history books had never even hinted at this sort of horror; never told him that hand-to-hand fighting with sharp weapons was such a disgusting and messy business, simply because one didn't have time to select the precise spot on one's opponent's head, limbs or torso at which to strike, slash, spike, or worse still, gouge. He smelt warm blood, and slipped on it.

They broke over the outer cashel quite soon in the proceedings, and farmers and monks alike beat hasty retreats to where their brothers were waiting to haul them up and over the middle wall. Nial was there, and Cailan too, a bit further along. Some never got to the wall; the Danes were as good at throwing their axes as they were at wielding them. Nial, helping to lift a young monk up over the rampart, felt him jerk, saw the sudden expression change in his brown eyes and the head loll sideways, and felt the hard, taut arm muscles slacken as the life left him.

'Drop him,' said the voice beside him.

'Drop him?'

'Yes.'

Nial dropped him, and for a moment stood lost and motionless. Then someone else was jumping up, and he was helping once more. He couldn't really see faces now.

He became aware of smoke; only a little at first, and then more and more until great clouds of it were drifting across the convulsing scene, and he heard above the shouts and the crashing, clattering, rattling row of the battle the crackle and roar of rioting flame. The School House roof, and that of the Cooking House next to it, were whirling skywards in a wild, gushing shower of sparks and leaping fire! Already the Danes were over the middle wall there, and he saw the vast figure of Ronan, the cook, laying about himself with a great knobbly club in one massive fist and the long and reddened blade of his best knife in the other. Nial saw an equally large Viking rise behind the sweating monk with up-raised sword, and calling a warning, he sprinted forward. There was a sudden, swift movement by the wall of the blazing school. Dichu's staff tripped the bulky raider with deftness and accuracy so that the whiskered face crashed on to a nearby stone. Another Dane sprang forward, and the lad's skinny back twisted and rippled as the young arms flexed and flashed, using the long pole, now as a shield intercepting the thrusting sword, and now as a cudgel across the swordsman's face so that the blood squirted from his shattered nose and he reeled off balance. A further flick and prod of the stick sent him crashing back against the nail-studded door of the burning school so that it gave way and fell inwards under him. Sparks whirled and flew. Yet another sheepskin-coated warrior appeared from the smoke, but almost in one movement Dichu skipped aside, and using his staff as a vaulting pole, virtually floated up on to the high bank of the innermost defence wall. And so Nial, unarmed, found himself face to face with the Dane. He saw the dark eyes bulging with battle-lust, saw the flash of the axe side-swiping towards him. He launched himself head-down into the hairy midriff, felt the strong arm slam across his shoulders as they fell. The sheep's wool stank. With the impetuous speed of desperation and revulsion, Nial wrenched himself to the side. It was not a considered move. Nor was his next one, but it took him in a flying leap after Dichu, and indeed, if it had not been for the slight but waiting arms of the boy, he would not have got over the rampart at all, and would have slipped back onto the figure below.

Dichu looked at him and grinned.

'I wish I was as handy as you are with a staff,' gasped Nial, swinging his feet down on to the stones. 'I could do with a weapon of some kind! Dichu! Look! There's Cailan! We've got to get him!'

The tattered, limping outline of Cailan, about four yards away, was lost for a moment in the driving smoke that billowed round the low buildings by the blazing Cooking House. When it cleared again he was standing with feet apart, facing a couple of broad, well-armed Vikings. Nial and Dichu jumped simultaneously. The small, rounded tip of the latter's staff, with the full weight of its owner's lithe body behind it, landed accurately and centrally just above the wide belt of the left-hand warrior. The staff broke and its splintered end disappeared into the man's side as he fell. Nial made an almost perfect rugger tackle on his man, knocking him forwards and down. He braced himself for the struggle. But nothing happened. The man died, choking. His own shield, now rocking round and round on the flagged pathway, had struck the ground edgeways on and his neck had come down across it, crushing the adam's apple.

Nial got up. The whirling axe-blade actually touched the side of his finger as it smacked into the ground! He sprang aside, something hit his head and he was reeling and staggering, with great bursts of light flashing up behind his eyes. He tripped, he fell; the earth was soft. Deep and soft.

Then he was being dragged. It didn't matter where. Or who by. It didn't hurt. He was being lifted. There were voices, gasping. He rolled. Downwards. All limbs and legs. A foot, bare and sinewy, stopped him. ''S all right,' someone said, and again: ''S all right,' and he realised it was himself who spoke. His eyes opened.

At first there were sparks. And then even as his consciousness grew he saw that they were real. Some of them swirled down on him and he felt them bite and sting on his legs.

Cailan was there, crouching beside him at the foot of the great wall. Fire filled the sky above him and it. Dichu was squatting with his back against the stonework, brushing away the smouldering ashes and flecks of burning straw that fell on his naked shoulders and thighs.

'Your hair's alight!' shouted Nial, and the youth flapped frantically at his long fair curls.

'Ach, Nial! And we thought you were dead!' Cailan's tender hand touched the top of Nial's head.

'Well, I'm not. Ooh!' He sat up, and Aendrum spun round, even with Cailan supporting him. His head buzzed and pounded.

'We must move, Mo-Nial. They will find us here!'

'Where are we, anyhow?'

'Just outside the middle wall,' Cailan shouted, over the roar of the flames. 'We did not try to get you into the inner cashel. It would be no use. The monastery cannot withstand them now!'

Dichu suddenly leapt up and started pulling Nial to his feet. 'Look, look!' he yelled. 'The school is collapsing!'

With the sound of a great wave bursting on a beach, the blazing roof crashed down into the inferno of the little building. Flame spouted from the window in the mud gable above them, and even as they scrambled from under it, a jagged crack appeared in the wall itself, widened, and part of the thing curled over towards them. They kept close under the cashel as they ran, crouched low. In a matter of yards they found their path barred by big clods of burning thatch which were sliding off the roof of what must be the Eating House. The heat blistered them as they skirted round, hoping they wouldn't be seen. Ahead, over the ridge of the drumlin, beyond the thick outer wall, and the static brown, white and pink lumps of the dead and dying, was the way to *Cuan*. There seemed no question about it. Cailan was heading that way.

'The boat, Dichu!' he was yelling. 'It is by the ford!'

They had only gone a dozen steps, when a shrill wailing swelled and crescendoed, stifled, and yet screaming in their ears. Halting, their turned eyes saw the flames lick orange death up the shingles of the church's distant roof. There was fire and smoke and consuming agony everywhere, but somehow this dug the fingers of pity deeper into Nial than everything else, for even he knew at once what the screaming was.

'My mother!' Dichu was off, running as though yanked along on the end of a string, straight for the wall.

'The women!' Cailan grabbed at Nial's shoulder. 'The women! They're in there with their babes!'

Nial was already out of his grasp and racing after Dichu. The squealing that rang out as he followed the scrambling naked boy over and through a broken gap in the rampart of sods urged him on, half in an attempt to stop Dichu from being silly.

They had to go round to the gateway beside the Bell House to gain entry to the inner cashel. They raced unscathed through groups of struggling, grappling men. Danes, farmers, monks; rolling, wrestling, stabbing. They jumped several bodies.

A terrible fight was going on at the gate: four or five raiders were trying to get through. One fell. Those on the other side were slashing and hewing at them with axes. Viking axes. Dichu paused, and Nial caught up and held him. One of the Danes slumped back, his face cleft down the middle. Another doubled up and crumpled; his sword dropped and lanced through the foot of a third. The axe caught *him* in the neck. It was then that Nial recognised Ranvaig and Shetelig as they hacked and cut, dodged and feinted in the narrow gateway. Recalling the mock-fights of their Viking boyhood when in the village of the Strong Fjord they played at 'going reeving' and sparred with wooden battle-axes, they fought well. Thanks to their monkly life, they were strong and far fitter than their opponents. But they were right out of practice.

The sword that cracked into Shetelig's temple held fast to his skull as he sagged and dropped, and was ripped from the hand that had swung it. The back edge of Ranvaig's axe smashed into the rib-cage of the disarmed man with such force and venom that he had to wrench it free.

Nial retched violently as he ran through the gap, side-stepping the groaning bodies. Dichu tore past him like the wind, and disappeared in the smoke. The grief-stricken expression that twisted Ranvaig's features as he looked up from his dead twin stopped Nial in his tracks.

'Is my brother, Nial! Oh, is my brother!' Ranvaig straightened, grabbed the torn hem of Nial's tunic, and stared into his face. 'Nial! Remember my brother when you go back to your time! Remember he made this warrior's death! Remember, and tell of it to you peoples! Shetelig! Oh, my Shetelig!' And he fell and hugged the ghastly wreckage to him, so that the fire glittered on the sword blade. And as he slumped further forward and let a long, groaning sigh spill from his hidden lips, Nial saw the broken-off shaft of the spear protruding from his back! He must have been fighting like that, he thought.

Standing there, motionless in the choking smoke, loneliness squeezed in on him from all sides, binding him into terrified helplessness on the spot. It was only the pleading, urgently calling voice floating down to him from the sky, that pulled him together.

'Son of Ross! Son of Ross!' Deeply and hoarsely it came down through the smoke. 'Nial! Nial of Aendrum!' Something in the last call seemed to burst within him, and he ran a step or two forwards—and saw the curving base of the Bell House. He felt rather than heard the fire rumbling within its frame. Its stone exterior seemed to tremble under his hand.

At his feet lay Aed, the bronze founder. Aed who had made Cailan's brooch. Aed who lay on his back with blood on his neck and beside him. Aed who was dead.

The voice came again, still patient, deep and controlled, and in a rush Nial recognised it for the Abbot's.

'Nial of Aendrum!'

'I'm here!' he yelled, staring upwards into the swirling, reeking smoke. 'I'm here!'

And in that moment he saw the falling object. It struck a stone at his feet with a noise which told him at once it was the Saint's bell. Its handle had fractured. It jangled briefly as he picked it up, and nearly fell again when the loose bit of handle broke right off. He got a hand to the clapper, which was tied loosely to it with a leather thong.

He had his mouth open to shout up when he saw another dark bundle land, on Aed's ample corpse. It rattled and clinked as it rolled off. Nial had no need even to consider what it was. He knew.

'Got them!' he shouted.

And high in the window of the Bell House, as the rushing heat tore up to engulf Abbot Sedna, the deep voice called out again, steadily, gladly, but with pain tightening each syllable: 'God speed you—Nial!'

There was nothing more to do. Grabbing up the clanking bag and hugging the bell to him, he sped back towards the gateway. Right in the very gap itself stood the small, red-haired Lief Thorsson. He had his back to Nial but was unmistakable even then. Nial skidded to a halt and heard the heavy bell sound dully as its clapper broke away and fell. Thorsson turned. Spinning round, and energised by sheer desperation, Nial sprinted along under the wall that doubled back towards Cailan's cell. He was hampered by the heavy bell. Everything about him seemed to be blazing; the clothing store was exploding into bulging clouds of flame. He could hear the pounding feet of the young Dane closing on him. The roof of the next hut had quite gone, leaving a smoking ring of stone wall, level with the cashel top. Nial sprang on to it, leapt for the edge, and jumped.

He landed very heavily on the pathway just in front of the smouldering remains of Cailan's little hut. There was the gateway on his left—and someone coming through it. The path led off to his right. Three Danes were pulling the contents out of one of the big huts there—they turned and saw him. Before him was the beehive-like structure of the old stone cell, with its gaping black doorway. For a moment, just a moment, Nial thought of diving in, barricading the entrance and . . . But even as Thorsson landed behind him he raced instead for the angle between it and the earthen top of the middle cashel, scrambling over and dropping into the outer enclosure. Around him were curving walls, and one or two small huts; ahead, the way to the herb garden. One hut was right beside him when he felt the cloth of the bag rip and become at once lighter in his hand. He clutched it to the side of his thigh and just prevented the most bulky object from falling out. To do even this he had to pause, and he saw the silver and bronze relic-box lying on the ground where it had dropped, Thorsson's long knife buried in its sheet-metal side. Its lid lay beside it, and the precious scroll of Gospels fluttered jerkily as though shuddering in the grass. Hitching up the remaining bundle, Nial sprinted on. It was only as he shot through the gateway at the end of the low wall that he glanced again over his shoulder.

The youth was bending greedily over the little box by the hut, with one hide-covered foot on the delicate scroll. He picked something up that twinkled, and Nial realised it was the ring of the Saint. He could do nothing, except take advantage of the situation. Again he dashed on, heading down for the gate in the outer cashel. And so it was that he did not see Bronach come from her hut with a heavy stone in her hands and bring it down with all her half-mad strength on the hateful shock of curly red hair before her. Nor, mercifully, did he see the approaching Dane who flung the spear that silenced her hysterical cackle.

Alone in Nial's mind was the thought of escape, and the words the Abbot had spoken to him quietly that night, up in the Bell House: '... if ever it should be in your power to make it possible for the cup to be preserved—do your very best ...' He could feel the thing in the crook of his arm as he stumbled on—it seemed to be rattling a bit. But broken or not, and although he had no idea how to, he was determined to save it if only because all else seemed lost. Again the memory of the deep voice boomed in his head: '... for other men— perhaps in other times ...'

The partly blocked gateway was before him. Darn bell, he thought. If only it still had its handle, or wasn't so heavy! The climb over the hurriedly heaped stones was difficult, to say the least. For one thing he had run almost completely out of energy—he'd had little enough to start all this with, anyway. He didn't dare look to see if he was still being followed until he was leaping down on the far side of the barrier. Just then there was no one in sight who appeared to be specifically chasing him. Mounting the stile over the little wall beyond the cashel proved impossible without the use of his hands to steady him. He laid the long bell carefully on its side and was himself astride the wall when he saw again the thick foliage of Bronach's garden beneath him. Without further thought he vaulted into it, dropped the brown bag at his feet, and lifting the bell, jumped with it to the angle formed between the connecting wall and the huge boulders of the cashel itself. Under the brilliant, tightly-packed marigolds he propped the bell mouth-down in the corner, and hastily piled one or two stones round it for further camouflage, with the idea of maybe coming back for it when the raiders had gone.

All was clear behind him as he swung himself up on to the stile again. The vault down to the grass of the open field beyond nearly finished him, for his legs were wobbly and weak. But, pulling a deep breath into his lungs and swallowing to lock it there, he held the bag to him and set off up the slope, heading as directly as he knew over the drumlin for the boat. As he crested the very top of the curve, he heard behind him above the yells in the background, the sort of shouts that could only mean he had again been seen, but in an instant the increasing downward slope was in his favour, speeding him on, panting now, pain glowing in his heart, and worse than that, the twinging agony of a stitch biting into his side. The last steep part of the hill was too much for his reduced control, and he tripped, sprawled, and crashed against the root of a thorn-tree, still clutching the bag. The figure that pounced on him almost made him faint in sheer fright.

'Ach, are you hurt?' Cailan seemed almost to scoop him up, but paused, staring. 'Mo-Nial! What is this you have?'

'Tholrykr's chalice; for God's sake take it! I'm done!'

'Saints! Nial! But the boat is just here, and almost afloat—I saw you jumping from the flames by the middle cashel and made straight for here, thinking you would arrive before I could, at my speed . . . ' He saw the oncoming Danes away above them. 'Come now, man!' And with one arm under Nial's shoulder and the other firmly clamped round the torn bag, he half-dragged him through the thorns and brambles and down over the stones and weed to where the little white *Cuan* lay waiting on the now falling tide. The wildly splashing water that rose from their slipping, fumbling feet refreshed Nial enough for him to jump in and get the oars shipped in their rowlocks, and Cailan dumped the priceless sack over the foredeck before shoving off and throwing himself after it.

Together on the rowing thwart they backed her swiftly out of the shallow water just as the two helmeted raiders came dashing along the stones from the direction of the ford. With a concerted heave they spun *Cuan* on her heel and with rapid, lengthening strokes, hove her through the water. It was almost like a recurring dream, the way the warriors took to the water in their wake, the two from the beach and now one, three, four more from the hill above, but this time it was clear to all that the boat was out of reach. Whirling and spinning, an axe came flying out after them. With the speed of an attacking bird it seemed to come curving down, right for Nial. In a jerking spasm he flung himself back—there was a quick 'Chunk'—and he saw Cailan smiling down at him and at the same time reaching over to retrieve his oar.

'A very fine movement,' came the soft voice, 'but if this thing had been sharper it would have cut the oar in two!'

Struggling up, Nial saw him wrench the wide blade from where it had struck—right between where his hands had been! Without thinking, he snatched the weighty weapon from Cailan's fist and in a white fury of rage he stood up and flung it at the wading Danes with every ounce of his strength. *Cuan* all but capsized—and the axe missed completely.

'Hmm . . . ' Cailan pulled him firmly but gently down on to the thwart. 'I understand of course, but I truly wish you had not done that. We could have done with a weapon. Look! They are going for their own boat to head us off!'

Pointing, and pushing each other on, the raiders were splashing back up over the seaweed and starting to sprint along the uneven shore to where, not very far ahead of them, Cedric Fairhead's great longship lay with her curving forefoot resting on the stones.

'Wait!' Nial backed violently on his oar, making *Cuan* swing hard round in her tracks. 'We'll head back for the ford!'

11

'Those who run away...'

There were barely a couple of inches of water over the mud and gravel of the ford, and *Cuan* was travelling so fast when she came to it that she drove half over before stopping. They leapt out, hove her on into the deeper water on the other side, and in a moment were rowing rapidly down the winding channel that eventually led eastwards along the north shore of the island. Close to starboard were the tall trees under which the two of them had first met, but beyond was the sound, the smell, the filth of death, tier upon tier of it by wall upon useless, defenceless wall, all crowned by the black smoke of ravaged, pillaged, destroyed Aendrum. And through the dark pall, rising like some grotesque firework that had failed to take off and was burning out in a spouting gush of flame, stood the slender, blazing finger of the round Bell House tower. Even as they watched, swaying strenuously to and fro at the oars, they saw a great portion at the top of it burst into a sudden spurt of flame and break off.

Cailan cried out as though his soul were falling with it.

Now the channel swept round more to the north-east, and the mud-flats were already drying out on either hand, but Nial felt the wind in his face and knew that even without the centre-plate they could sail. As they swung the oars in-board and he bent over the transom to ship the rudder, that same wind brought the smoke swirling down about them, and to their ears the moans, the dreadful, ghastly moans of the wounded.

And ashes, small whitish specks and particles, fell fluttering and flittering softly about them.

They hadn't the strength to get the sail properly hoisted, but it didn't really matter. The breeze gained strength as they slid away from the holocaust astern, and the ebb tide gathered speed under them, too. Then, as they made swiftly along the coast of the island, they saw the other fires; the mud and wicker huts of the farmers, their sheep pens, their crops, their animals being systematically destroyed. ruined. That didn't matter much either, really. It was very doubtful if anyone was left who could tend them—the Danes would not, for sure.

It was all of a mile to the end of the island, and they had covered most of that before Nial suddenly said: 'Where are we going?'

'Going?—I—I have not the least—unless—no, I—do not—' Cailan's voice trailed away, and they sailed on.

Just before rounding the long, low, eastern tip of Mahee, it occurred to Nial that if the big longship *had* been launched, she would probably be out in the open lough, watching for them. So putting his helm up, he luffed *Cuan* round behind the little islet now known as Bird Island, and ran her nose up into the grey mud. With the sail and mast lowered to make them less conspicuous, they stayed there for the remaining hour or two of daylight, with the nauseating smell of smoke wafting past them.

The sun set, spreading rosy light into the western sky over Reagh Island opposite. Sea-birds and waders came down to the pale water and left their footprints on the glistening, pimply mud. The wind eased to a mere air, and in a while the tendrils of smoke that rose from the reeking wreckage of Mahee streamed slowly upwards in silent, unwavering spirals, tinted pink and purple in the dying light. Some last distant shouts were heard, and the blowing of a horn which no doubt rallied the victorious Vikings to their departing ships.

'They will carry their dead away—' said Cailan, his voice low and still. 'They will give them a hero's burial on the island down in the Narrows by their settlement. They will have robbed our poor people and left them to rot before the eyes of our God.'

Nial looked over to the far-away ruins. 'Then we can go back and try to bury them! Come on!' And without really thinking of what he had suggested, he began to lift the oars clear of the lowered sail.

'Ach, no, Mo-Nial!' Cailan's thin, almost delicate hand touched his arm, and quite firmly pressed it down. 'We must not go back!'

'Not? But why? Surely there is no one else who can...'

'Ah, but there will be, my friend. There are those who always run away—more than just ourselves. There is no blame in that, for it is themselves who will return and do the burying. But not for a day or two—maybe a week. It will not be a pleasant job. But for the moment, the Danes are still there.'

'I thought I heard—aren't they on their way home?'

'The most of them are, no doubt, but have you forgotten what they came for? Some will stay to catch those who creep back too soon, or those who hid and are forced into the open in search of water, and they will be taken and—and made to tell where the treasure lies.'

'But they cannot know! We have that.'

'Some of it, yes, and the best, thanks to God. And the Danes themselves will have whatever brooches and pins and fine things they have ripped from those they have murdered.'

He looked Nial squarely in the eyes. 'You think that will stop them questioning?'

'Maybe not; but surely if there is nothing—'

'Those that they ask will answer something, or die.'

'But if they say there *is* some hidden, they will only be found out. Won't that be the worse for them?'

'Ach, indeed not! They will die anyway, just as soon as they have spoken at all.'

Nial was searching his over-tired brain for something to say, some word, some way of comforting not just his friend, but himself too, when he heard the sucking noise. The dusk clung low to the islet's shore and all was shade. He could see nothing. He found himself clutching Cailan's scrawny forearm, and felt the hairs prickle at the back of his neck.

The noise again; uneven, pausing; sucking as only mud can suck and squelch under the feet of a human being! And then they saw him. Round the stony end of the islet, thin, dirty, slipping, staggering, with waving arms and a naked young body, came Dichu. He fell flat only five feet from the boat, and by the time they got him aboard, they were all liberally smeared with the glutinous slime. Cailan hugged the bony, slippery lad to him, and even Nial found himself calling him 'Mo-Dichu' and joyfully holding a small muddy hand, while sheer relief forced tears of gladness from his eyes.

When Dichu was at last able to talk, he told how he had got the women—his mother and baby sister among them—safely from the blazing church just before the roof started to fall in. Then as they fled for the east gateway, through the reception enclosure, they had found themselves running into a trap. Urged by his mother, Dichu had escaped by climbing a pillar on to the already burning roof of a lean-to shed, and jumping down from the cashel wall. Twice before he got clear away he was grabbed by raiders.

'But,' he said, 'my skin is smooth and I am quick.' The dull red and purple bruises on his arms, thighs, and the back and sides of his little torso which showed between the smears of mud, eloquently told the rest of the tale. Much of his long hair had been singed away, and there was an angry red burn on one shoulder.

'I saw you sail this way,' he continued, 'so when I got out—' he shuddered, paused, and went on, 'I—came this way. It was only a thought that brought me out to this island, here—you see, I ran, Cailan,—I ran away! I thought they wouldn't find me out here—' he began to sob. 'Trichem was with me as we climbed the outer wall—they held on to him by his cloak—me too—but I got away, and ran.' He looked from one to the other, his eyes wide, wet and red-rimmed. Then bursting into an avalanche of bitter tears, he turned and stared out over the still water to the far-away hills. 'I saw what they did to him!' he croaked.

Soon afterwards, Nial remembered the brown bag, and thought it would cheer the boy up a bit to know that the contents were safe. It did much more than that, for it turned out that Dichu had only seen the chalice twice before—and then with the full length of the church between him and it.

When Nial held the gleaming cup up to examine it in the half light, its smooth, curved belly, its gold and jewels winked and twinkled, so Dichu could barely believe his eyes. Neither could Nial, for there was no sign of damage at all.

In the bag also was the big silver ring-brooch with the prickly-knobbed ends, and it had been this that Nial had heard rattling against the chalice. It was also undamaged, except that the long pin was just a trifle bent.

'The relic-box fell out, Cailan.' Nial felt he ought to explain, for he was sure his friend would wonder why it was not there. Then a new thought struck him.

'What'll we do with the chalice, Cailan? Who do we take it to?'

Cailan gazed at him in the fading light. 'Do? Take it to? I have not thought. Will you not keep . . . '

'Oh, no! If I can get it to some responsible person in a safe place, I shall feel I have done my job! I once said I would do my best for its safety—but I wouldn't call *Cuan* exactly free of risk, and I have nowhere else to put it.'

Cailan suddenly straightened. 'I know, Nial! Of course! Uncle Dairmid at Inchcleraun! We will take your boat up the river at the head of the lough! The monks at Commar will look after it for you. Then we can set off to find Uncle Dairmid! It is a very long journey from here to Lough Ree, but *he* will guard the chalice, if anyone can!'

'That sounds fine,' said Nial. 'I don't mind the walk.'

'It will not be easy; but we can stop to rest at the many establishments of the Church along the way. With such a burden we will have to take as few risks as possible.'

Dichu turned. 'We could travel at night, maybe! Then the Danes would not see us.'

'Don't you be so sure,' muttered Nial, remembering the escape from Strangford. 'But in a while we'll give it a try.'

And around them the world sank into the deepening, and apparently more peaceful shades of night.

In time it was fully dark, but for the dim lingering after-glow in the north-western sky. Gradually the breeze came again, gently at first, and the silver edge of the new tide came flooding slowly in over the cold, hissing mud, its flat wet fingers poking this way and that on the uneven surface. Tiny creatures began to stir as it approached, and small crabs scuttled along the side of the boat, tap-tapping their shells against the thin planking. Other unseen things blew little bubbles up through the incoming water, and Nial and Cailan quietly set about stepping the mast and making sail.

It was the same breeze, from the west-south-west, lightish, but good and steady, under a gathering pall of black cloud.

It was the same longship, that they had last seen on the shore of battle.

She was some way off, lying darkly, deadly, close by the long spit at Mahee's eastern tip. As *Cuan* slid clear of the tiny islet, Dichu, watching from the bows, saw the low outline. The way up the open lough was barred.

There was only the one thing Nial could do. Slamming the tiller down, he swung *Cuan* round, and held her hard on the wind back up towards Aendrum.

It began to rain; huge thundercloud drops that plunked into the water singly at first, then more and more until it was hissing down, drenching them. They ran aground, unable to see more than a few feet. They struggled through the mud, hauling *Cuan* between them—and soon found themselves wading on to the harder footing of the ford. There was not yet water enough to cover it, and the boat was heavy. Somehow they got her over, slid her gratefully down the mud beyond, and with a final shove, leapt in as she floated. The rain had hidden them from any watchers. And only the rain on that pitch black night made them accidentally run the boat aground a second time.

Where they were, they did not know. There was only one way to find out. Clambering wearily once more over the side, they scrambled up over the weeds, Dichu still hugging the sodden treasure bag, and Nial dragging *Cuan*'s painter, so that he could tie her to a boulder while they scouted round. Crossing a tangle of driftwood at the high-water mark, he felt his foot catch under something, and flung out his arms as he fell. The world burst into a great explosion of brilliant, dazzling, intermingling lights, all colour, dancing, flickering, fading, fading, fading . . .

12

'Perhaps in other times...'

He became aware of his skin.

It was stiff, almost thick.

And terribly, terribly cold.

His face was on grass, flattened under his heavy cheek. His head didn't lift when he first tried it, so he left it there for a while longer.

Both arms were like lead, but he found he could move his fingers a little. Then, as he got a leg moving and the cold burned into him, he realised that he was stark naked. His tunic had gone! With stiff eyes opening to the grey dawn-light, he raised himself uncertainly on to his elbows. Everything was still, silent, held down like himself by the icy chill of the morning air. And then a tern colony in the distance sprang into shrill chittering life, and he saw *Cuan* just a few yards back along the beach, her tall mast tilting, and the thin halyards curving down to the limp, hanging folds of the lowered sail. At his feet were a scattering of bleached, sea-washed branches.

He sat up, sore in every joint, and shivering violently. Where his tunic was, he couldn't think, but there beside him in the grass, the twinkling bronze ring-brooch caught his eye. He picked it up. It *had* been pinned into his woven belt, he remembered. But that had gone, too. He stared at the brooch. Cailan! Dichu! Where were they? He glanced rapidly round ... and found himself staring across the water at the clean, white, rectangular shape of a cottage on the distant shore!

A cottage? Wildly his heart jumped and banged against his ribs; wildly he looked up the hill behind him. Trees . . . and the top of a ruined farmhouse! So it *had* been a dream! And yet . . . Across the chill grey of the water lapping the stones just below him—far across—the unmistakable shattered stump of Nendrum's ancient round tower and the pale lines of the broken walls capped the nearest island! He leapt to his feet—and staggered at the pain of them!

Somehow he hobbled down to *Cuan*. She had dew on her gunwale, and water in her bilges. He stared about him again. Not a soul was in sight. Not Cailan, nor Dichu . . . he wouldn't expect them now! But the little brooch was there, in his fist. Hauling in the painter, he shoved the boat out into more weed-free water. Shuddering with cold, he settled to the oars—noting that one of them was indeed nearly cut through—and he headed as quickly as he could down towards the gap between Rainey and Mahee. The tide was just ebbing and no more, but it didn't take him long. As he turned the boat round the end of Rainey and towards the fleet of moored yachts in Whiterock Bay, the sun lifted clear of the distant Ards shore.

He could feel the warmth of it on his chest and stomach—his very, very empty stomach . . .

Sitting on the top deck of the bus that lurched and rumbled its way towards the outskirts of Belfast, and feeling more human after finding himself some dry clothes and a quick breakfast on the yacht, he was so engrossed in the thoughts of what he had seen and experienced that he did not even notice the curious glances that his fellow passengers gave to his extremely grubby and badly bruised face. Their gaze would drop eventually to the knee-boots and the battered and mildewed duffle-bag, and back up to his tangled, matted dark hair. And it suited him that no one sat beside him. He was seeing the familiar passing landscape with new eyes; eyes that noted, wondered, and appreciated. Brick and concrete houses, the metalled road, telegraph poles, the bus windows, cars, a motor-bike; and things that hadn't changed at all; birds and a brown scurrying rat, trees, grass.

The noise and speed of travel dinned and hammered on his ears in continual clamour. How peaceful, in a way, was the world he had left behind in the night. Peaceful?

And then a horrible thought exploded in his mind and made his ears blush pink with the suddenness of its occurrence: the chalice! He was sure enough that he had not seen it when he came to on the shores of Wood Island that morning—but he hadn't really looked! Suppose it was still there! He wanted to get off the bus and go back. He half turned in his vibrating seat before realising that there was no point.

He made himself think again. Why complicate the issue? If the brown bag was there—supposing he really hadn't imagined its existence—then the chances of it being picked up during the day were still somewhat remote. Surrounded by mud at low tide, Wood Island was anyway privately owned. No one lived there, and as far as he knew it was rarely visited. And an old brown bag would not be exactly conspicuous. His father would surely come with him, and they would hunt for it. His father . . . And staring out down the long road ahead, Nial wondered how on earth he would start to tell his story. Just as at first he himself had failed to believe what was happening, he could see how very much less likely, particularly in the real twentieth century, it was all going to seem, even to his own parents. Only the little bronze ring-brooch in the pocket of his jeans would go some of the way to help. He put his hand down and felt it through the thin cloth.

As it happened, his father came home for lunch that day. He did not usually manage this on a Thursday, but things had been a bit slack at the office, and there he was, driving in at the gate just as Nial came round the corner from the bus-stop.

In the event, both parents were so appalled at the general appearance of their son that they ordered him up to the bath practically on sight. It was glorious too, sitting there in the steaming water, soaping away the mud and blood and discovering just how many scratches and cuts and bruises he in fact had; and it was while he was thus engaged that his father came in and sat himself on the bath-stool. What had Nial been up to? And in fact, with hardly any prompting at all, Nial was soon outlining the whole affair.

John Ross listened, increasingly puzzled, but showing neither amusement nor disbelief on his face, until Nial, covered in soap, told him to take the little pin from the pocket of the jeans that lay crumpled on the floor. He studied the bronze brooch carefully and long, lines of concentrated thought crinkling the edges of his eyes. Then he looked down at Nial, at the great bluish bruise on the boy's forehead, the cuts on his shoulder, arms and feet.

'Your Mum'll have lunch ready,' he said, getting up. 'Better come on down.'

Nial could hear him talking away in the kitchen directly below, as he got himself dried and dressed. How strange the trousers felt!

Lunch was a funny meal. Nial ate rather too much for comfort, though his mother seemed surprised at his refusing a second helping of white peaches and custard. He did what he could to answer their questions, and often saw them look at one another, not with knowing sort of looks, so much as utterly mystified ones.

At last his father looked directly at him, seriously.

'You aren't making this up, are you.' It was more of a statement than a question, but the need for an answer was there. For just a moment Nial was silent, hunting in the corners of his mind for—oh, traces of a dream, perhaps. His father's steady gaze was deep and searching. He met it.

'No, Dad. At least . . . I really don't think I am. These bruises—well, I just don't know how else I got them—and really they're jolly sore! Unless . . . It *is* Thursday, isn't it?'

'Yes.'

'Well, in that case—if I wasn't doing—I mean, if I wasn't *there*, with the monks and Vikings and—and so on, I—well I can't remember having done anything else since Sunday morning. I'm sorry. It's weird, I know.'

'Weird! Somewhat understating it, aren't you? Do you honestly realise what you're saying?'

'Yes, Dad. Look, I—I can't explain it, not even to myself!'

'Well, we can only take your word for it, son, though you're asking a hell of a lot of us! But I must say, if you *have* no other explanation for those bruises and cuts, I confess I don't know what else to think, myself. Your descriptions are remarkably vivid. Otherwise I would have said you had somehow dreamed the whole thing, real and all as it may seem to you. On the other hand, I know you're not given to scrapping with strangers. Or anyone else for that matter. Nor would that explain the cuts, particularly those on your feet. Did you put dressings on them after your bath?'

'The biggest ones, yes.'

'Hmm . . .' Mr Ross paused, and rubbed the tip of his nose lightly with the knuckle of his forefinger. 'You know, what beats me is why you should be so insistent about such an unlikely yarn! Not that the details themselves are unlikely—we know at least some of them are fact.'

Nial sat up keenly. 'Which ones?'

'Oh, well, the date for one thing, and Abbot O'Deman—there are written records about him. Oh, and when they were excavating at Nendrum in the twenties, they did find skeletons that would tally nicely—look, you haven't been mugging this up from the book, have you?'

'Dad! I didn't even know there *was* a book! Can't you see . . . ? Oh, but *who* did they find?'

'Whose skeletons, you mean? Well, their names aren't recorded, of course, but there *was* once a Norse Abbot with a gammy leg. Come to that, there were also two strongly constructed Norse skeletons in one of the burial heaps, one of whom had, I think the report said, died from a sword cut in the head.'

'Horrible,' said Mrs Ross, 'but I remember reading that myself.'

'It's true,' nodded Nial. 'I saw—it. Did you say "burial heap", Dad?'

'Yes. It seems some of the locals must have come back after the raid and piled all the bodies together and covered them over with earth—to stop the smell, I suppose.'

'John! Must you?'

'Sorry dear, but the lad wanted to know. Tell you a strange thing about that, too. One of the skeletons—young woman, I think she'd been—had had a trephining operation. Hole bored in her skull, you know. She'd lived for quite a time after it, too.'

'Bronach.' Nial's face was blank and expressionless. 'I told you—she grew their herbs for them.'

'Good heavens! You mean you met her?' His mother stared, coffee-pot poised.

'Yes, of course. Now do you believe me?'

'I'm beginning to think I have to, Nial! Even if it *should* all be impossible and preposterous. But that brooch must have come from somewhere, and it looks perfectly genuine to me, yet not at all weathered.'

'You sure you didn't just find it?' His father picked up the object from the table, and weighed it again in his hand.

'I'm not sure I can be sure about anything. Dad, I can only believe what I *felt* happening—and I told you, Aed ... Oh, darn it, I *know* Cailan gave it to me!'

'This "treasure", Nial,' asked his mother after a while, 'the thing you or this lad had at the end of it all; it was a sort of chalice, you say?'

Nial described it, as closely as he could.

His parents glanced at each other. 'Well,' said his father, 'I know what that sounds like, though of course it can't be, not unless it was found a very long way from home.'

'How do mean, Dad?'

'Well, never mind that now. I think all this justifies me taking the afternoon off. Bill's quite capable of holding the fort at the office on his own. We are going to drive down to Nendrum and talk this over on the spot—provided the causeway is back to normal—*and* we'll call in at the Museum on the way home. What else did you say the Abbot gave you?'

'He didn't exactly *give* me anything. He had some idea that I would be able to save it for posterity—anyway, he just dropped it and hoped I would pick it up. Look, it may sound funny, but it wasn't a bit. There were people being killed all round me! Swords and axes are messy things.'

Walking over the quiet, lichen-grown ruins, which appeared

to his parents much as they did on their previous visit a few years earlier, Nial felt strange. He simply couldn't stop himself almost constantly looking back over his shoulder, as though afraid of—he knew not what. When a cow which was chewing the cud down by the outer cashel suddenly mooed loudly he positively jumped.

'Ghosts chasing you?' His father spoke gently, not poking fun.

'A bit,' said Nial, and put his hand on the rough stones of the inner cashel near where the old stone cell of Saint Mohee had stood. Under his feet was grass, now. But under that grass was the paved pathway once trodden by Cailan, Finnian, Cathal, and the rest of them. Now—stillness.

'What else was in your treasure bag, apart from the chalice?' asked his mother, quietly.

'Oh, well a sort of ornate box like a house, and full of what they called "relics", a simply fabulous scroll-thing among them; but the Danes got all that. Then there was this old bell effort. Its handle broke when the Abbot threw it down to me . . . Mum, he was burning alive up there! It was horrible!'

'I would think it probably was.' Janet Ross spoke slowly, her face tight with the thought of what her son seemed to have lived through. She knew the contents of the Museum in Belfast very well. She knew of the battered old bell that had been dug up in a corner by one of the cashel walls when 'Nendrum' was excavated in the early twenties. She had been just a little girl then, and that kind of thing was only exciting to old fogies who collected fossils and the like. Since then, however, she had seen the bell with its broken handle, and the display cabinets filled with other finds from the site. And some of them at least, she was sure Nial had quite unwittingly described during lunch that afternoon.

It was a long time since Nial had been to the Museum. When he had gone in the past, it was to find the exhibits merely curious, rather than interesting. To him, archaeology had always seemed something of a waste of time. How anyone could get worked up about things that were out of date centuries ago—a lot of old flints and broken pots and so forth—when the whole of the modern world lay there outside the hushed windows of the great silent galleries, had been quite beyond him.

Now, for the first time, he had a very real reason to be interested. But for all this, he was not in any way ready for his own reaction when his parents led him into the 'Early Christian' section of the building.

Near the doorway was part of a grave-slab with a cross cut in it. Under the stone, appropriately indeed, was a plaque bearing the simple word; 'Nendrum'. Nial realised it was one of those that had once paved and decorated the church floor. There were also many carved crosses and things from other early ecclesiastical sites in the country. Stones; a little pottery; a rusty sickle and the decayed remains of small articles from the period.

There too, was a model that somebody had made of what they thought the site of Nendrum had once looked like, but it was empty, so empty, in comparison to the crowded, cluttered place that Nial had seen.

But perhaps the worst thing of all—the thing that made his forehead prickle with little icy beads of sweat, that made him draw a sharp breath and hold hard on to the edge of the case, was a display of 'trial pieces' of slate, dug out of the remains of what had been the School House. There, in one corner, Nial instantly recognised the very piece that young Dichu had held out to him before breakfast on his first morning at Aendrum. There, fresh as on that very day, were the little scratched-on knotwork patterns and the small and beautiful intersecting circles drawn by Trichem. He saw too the donkey pulling the squarish tilling device, and with an even stronger pang of remembrance, the little picture of the strange, twisted horse whose artist had turned it so that it would fit into the limited space of the stone. There were these, and much more. At the end of the case were some small 'ring-pins' and brooches; bronze, most of them; and one at least was quite plainly the work of Aed. He put his hand in his pocket, and bringing out Cailan's little penannular brooch, he held it close to the glass of the case, near the others.

Even to his parents' eyes, there was no doubt about its origin. Nial looked at the collection, silently. His mother watched him, and knew.

John Ross put his hand gently on his son's shoulder. 'Anything else in this room that you recognise?'

There was an aerial photograph of Nendrum, showing the neat lines of the re-discovered walls and foundations—the cashels stood out very clearly, as did the church and the stump of the Bell House—he could see the rectangular outline of the School House, the Cooking House, the round little workshops—'That's where the brooch was made,' he said, pointing to one of them.

Suddenly his heart leapt and his legs went weak. Standing there among a row of similar ones from other sites was the Bell of Nendrum itself. Though it was much corroded, and blackened all over by some conservation treatment, there was no mistaking it. Its broken handle seemed to pull at him. He remembered the feel of it as he struggled to hide it by the cashel wall. And here it was again, safe after all those ages ...

Just as he was about to leave, Nial noticed on the left a

brightly-lit case. It seemed to contain some highly-ornamented gold crosses and relic shrines, some of which were almost as elaborately decorated and worked as—as—but—there it was!

'Dad!' His shout rang and echoed in the huge hall, and he cared not at all. 'That's it! That's the chalice!'

There, in the very centre of the case, slightly tarnished, but mounted over a mirror so that one could see the glowing curves of the rock-crystal under its squat, conical base; there, complete with all its profusion of gold twists and squirls and criss-crosses, was Abbot Tholrykr's chalice.

Mr Ross smiled broadly as he put an arm round Nial's shoulders. 'I thought as much!' he said. 'But I wanted to see if you would recognise it. Actually, and I'm sorry to disappoint you, but that one there is only a facsimile of the real one, which is kept in Dublin. Would you say it was a good copy?'

'Good!' There was no regret in Nial's voice, nor in his mind. 'It's so good I was sure it was the cup itself! Oh, Dad!' Nial let his eyes soak in the brilliance of the detailed workmanship that glittered and sparkled under the strong lights of the display case. Why, even the faintly stippled-in band with the names of the Apostles was clearly reproduced, and he knew that whoever had made this copy had lovingly held in his hands the very article that he himself had lifted out of the tattered brown bag in *Cuan* just last night. Last night? Or all but a thousand years ago?

Below the chalice was a card saying where the original had been found.

Nial was bewildered. He had never heard of the place.

His mother stood beside him, tears filling her eyes, though she couldn't think why. 'They found it and a big ring-brooch, in a circular earthwork that was being ploughed up or something. It's somewhere away down in the middle of Ireland.'

Nial felt the flash of realisation jump within him. Perhaps, oh, just perhaps, after all—but his father was thinking ahead of him.

'Seems like your young monk and his little friend had quite a walk!'

'Dad! Is that—could it possibly be *anywhere* near—Lough Ree, I think he said?'

'Who said?'

'Cailan. He had an uncle who was Abbot of a monastery on one of the islands there! Oh, Dad, is it near?'

'It is indeed, my lad! Not much over ten miles away, I should think.'

And suddenly Nial was immensely happy.

Cailan had got there, after all. How he had found his way off Wood Island he would never know, but there could be little doubt about it. Cailan had gone to his uncle! And if that was so, then probably Dichu, too, had survived. *And* the chalice; the chalice still existed! Who cared if they called it something else? It was the sheer glory of the object itself that mattered!

And once again, the words of Abbot Sedna rang in his mind: 'For the cup to be preserved for other men—perhaps in other times—to see, to wonder at, to think on . . .'